I0623024

Lux in Tenebris: Poena et Salus

ISAAC RYALS

THE WHUMPY PRINTING PRESS

ALSO BY ISAAC RYALS

The Honor Bound Series

CONTENTS

CONTENT WARNINGS

This story contains the following content:

- Themes related to Judeo-Christian religion, including angels, demons, references to possession and exorcism, and quotes from scripture.

- Kidnapping

- Recapture

- PTSD

- Restraints, collar, gag

- Torture

- Blood

- Character death

If this book isn't for you, no worries! But if it is, we hope you enjoy this story about a hapless demon...

1

— · —

The iron cuffs burned Dee's wrists. His shoulders ached from his hands being locked behind him. He twisted weakly against the restraints, his heart lying sluggish and still in his chest, barely able to breathe the stuffy air in the car's trunk. The car went over a bump, and he bit back a cry of pain as his head thudded against the lid of the trunk, then the floor. The trunk was warded, he could feel it: the familiar prickle of power cloaking him from anyone who might be looking for him. Tears streamed down his cheeks and into the cloth gag tied around his head.

He could hear the angels in the car as they laughed and turned up their music. It grated on his ears, tinny guitar and crashing drums, but at least it covered the sound of their cruel laughter. He whimpered softly and pressed his face against the rough carpet on the floor.

His stomach heaved. It was going to happen again. He felt the weight of his capture so many years ago – out at the bar, having a good time in the woman's body he had borrowed, reveling in the life and music and joy that humans could feel when they

2

allowed themselves to. He remembered the room beginning to swim around him. He remembered the Power that had stepped forward – but he hadn't known it was a Power, how could he when he was drunk with the colloidal silver they'd spiked his drink with? – with gloved hands, smiling at the demon as he stumbled away from the bar.

"Hey, sweetie, had a little too much to drink, huh? Yeah, baby, let's go home."

He vaguely remembered the bartender watching him as he was pulled toward the exit, just a flash of doubt crossing the bartender's face, a moment of hesitation – before someone had called for another round of shots, and he'd turned away to grab the shot glasses. Dee remembered staggering out the door to the bar, tucked under the Power's arm – protected by his gloves and long sleeves, how could he have *missed* that?

He remembered being shoved to his knees in the alley behind the bar. He remembered the cuffs being clicked around his wrists, remembered being thrown into the trunk of a car, remembered the jolt as the car began to move ...

He remembered waking up in a basement with an iron collar around his neck and iron cuffs around his wrists, shaking his head against the cacophony of sobbing inside his head. He remembered the woman screaming from the pain, from the burning in her wrists, from the fear as one of the Powers stepped up – there were more of them now, three standing in a circle around them – and took the demon's face in his hand.

In his ungloved hand.

The car hit another bump, and this time Dee couldn't choke back the sob as he slammed against the floor of the trunk again. Another spike of laughter from the car. Tears streamed down Dee's face.

Dee. The name Ilya had given him.

He tossed his head and lurched forward, desperately pulling up the face of his kind human friend in his mind. He keened softly as he remembered their soft voice, their gentle hands, their quiet way as they held him tight and rocked him and slept beside him in bed, asking nothing from him, a warm presence that steadied him, cared for him.

Loved him, maybe.

They can't know about Ilya.

He clenched his jaw shut, shuddering from the blistering pain in his wrists, from the fear, from the ache in his chest that opened up inside him and threatened to swallow him whole. He could remember how it felt when the human in his body screamed and suffered alongside him. He could remember how it felt when he woke after being drowned in holy water and realized he could no longer hear her voice in his head.

The Powers killed a human, just so they could torture a demon.

They would not get Ilya.

His stomach roiled, and he gagged against the cloth in his mouth. He could feel the angelic hands on his body, could feel how his skin blistered and burned from even the slightest touch – not like the slow, stinging pain of the iron, but an instant flame, charring his skin, blackening it. He could feel the whip, the blinding agony as it shredded his back, lash after lash until his flesh hung from his bones. He could feel the white-hot blade of the knife, consecrated iron burning into his skin, poisoning his blood. A knife that would kill him if the angels cut too deep, the only hope of escape he had.

He bleated in fear, sick with the pain that crashed through his body with each memory. They would break him all over again. They would hurt him and hurt him and hurt him until there was nothing left, nothing but a shell – like he had been when Dara carried him away from that hell months ago.

Tears streamed from his eyes as he desperately hoped Dara would come for him again. He pleaded silently that she and Evangeline would save him before the Powers took everything from him. They weren't like the other angels – they cared, impossible though it seemed. If Dara couldn't save him, the only thing he could hope for – could beg for – was that the Powers took his life.

His skin crawled as the car slowed to a stop. The car bounced slightly as the Powers climbed out. Dee felt the jolts as they each slammed their doors shut.

The trunk lid opened, and he blinked against the sudden light. He cringed back from the angels' hands as they reached in and pulled him from the trunk. He sobbed weakly as they dragged him forward, shoving him toward the front door of a house at the end of a long driveway. He couldn't see another house in any other direction. As he approached the door, his heart sank.

There was a warding symbol on the door, just like he had felt on the trunk – and just like Evangeline had drawn on the front door of Ilya's house. Dara and Evangeline would never find him now. He would disappear into that house, be chained to the floor, be torn apart for however long the Powers wished to hold him.

He began to sob in earnest as they dragged him through the front door.

2

Dee shrieked in terror as the angels dragged him toward the open basement door. His shoes squeaked and slid on the wood floor, and tears streamed into the gag as he twisted away from the Powers. His sweat-soaked clothes ripped under the angels' hands. His heart lay silent within him, even as his chest heaved with terrified gasps.

"Fucking *filth*," an angel spat. A hand lashed across Dee's face, leaving blistering skin in its wake. Dee sobbed and shuddered as his tears stung the burn. The door to the basement yawned open, the peeling gray walls of the staircase disappearing down into blackness.

"*P-please*," he gasped, the word muffled by the gag. "*Please, no, please, mercy –* " His eyes were wide, helpless, as he looked around at his captors. He remembered their names; they were burned into his mind at the point of a knife, at the end of a whip, seared into his soul. He knew their names better than he knew his own.

Lucas. Jude. Dominic.

Their faces were all twisted with hate, their inhuman beauty poisoned by their twisted mouths, their spiteful eyes. He could barely breathe as they dragged him to the basement door and shoved him forward.

He almost caught himself on the first stair, the impact shuddering through his sneakers. Then he felt a boot in his back, and he pitched forward into blackness.

The fall seemed to last an eternity.

When he hit the floor, his shoulder buckled and his skull cracked against the cement in a brilliant flash of light. The rest of his body followed in a boneless heap. For a breath, there was no sensation in his body but blank, dizzying terror.

The pain rushed in a moment later.

He screamed his throat raw. Agony shuddered up and down his arm, dull and crushing and nauseating. He gagged weakly and sobbed, rolling onto his other side and curling into himself as much as he could. His shoulder screamed at him as he pulled against the iron cuffs locking his hands behind him. Sweat chilled on his skin. His teeth began to chatter.

Above the sound of his screams, he could hear the angels laughing. A single lightbulb clicked on above him, casting the basement in stark, yellowed light. His vision swam as the angels descended the steps one by one and gathered around him where he lay shuddering. The light stabbed into his eyes as he looked up at them. He squeezed his eyes shut, sending more tears dripping onto the cement floor.

His eyes flew open again as a boot drove into his stomach. He let out a choked, gurgling scream. The fractured bones in his shoulder ground together, seeming to spark a fire that roared under his skin. He felt more than saw the Trap painted on the floor around him, severing any change of escape from his body – even if he had the strength to exorcize himself.

"Looks like we found our little snake out in the grass," Lucas murmured, crouching down and reaching out to touch Dee. "Here we thought we'd never see our little serpent again."

"*N-no*," Dee heaved. Black spots floated in his vision. If the angel touched him, he was going to be sick, he was going to *die* ...

Lucas drew one finger down Dee's cheek. The skin sizzled under the touch, and Dee jerked his head away, sobbing and shaking and pleading wordlessly. Jude dropped to his knees behind Dee and jerked his head back. The smell of burning hair was acrid in Dee's nostrils.

"When that little Virtue pulled you out of our basement, we thought we *lost* our little sinner, didn't we?" Lucas crooned. The others laughed in agreement. "Who'd have thought we would find it months later, walking around like it was *human*?"

"Walking with a little limp, though, huh?" Dominic said through his cheerfully clenched teeth. He crouched beside Lucas. "Those legs never did heal right, did they?"

"I want to take this off," Lucas said, eyeing the gag. With Jude keeping Dee's head steady with the hand in his slowly singeing hair, Lucas dragged his finger down Dee's cheek again – and pulled the gag from his mouth.

"*P-please*," Dee wailed, desperately locking his muscles tight and hoping his shivering would ease. It only made him tremble harder. "Please – mercy, Powers, please, *obsecro, potestates, obs-se-cro, non, miserere mei, misericordia –* " [*Please – mercy, Powers, please, please, Powers, p-please, no, have mercy on me, mercy –*]

A slap lashed across his face and knocked his head against the cement again. His ears rang with the force of it.

"*Quia lingua non est tibi*" [*This language is not for you*], Lucas snapped. "*Sordes damnatus*" [*Damned filth*].

"*I-ignosce me*" [*F-forgive me*], Dee sobbed desperately, his mind a jagged slash of panic. "*Tantum volo misericordia, obsecro, obsecro –* " [*I only want mercy, please, please –*]

Lucas shoved him onto his back, put his knee on his chest, and *leaned.* His hands were crushed under him and the bones crunched in his shoulder. Dee's head fell back against the floor and he screamed in agony.

"*Non venenum lingua nostra per tuus oris turpis*" [*Don't poison our language with your filthy mouth*], the angel snarled in his face. Dominic got to his feet with a smirk, disappearing into the circle of darkness that surrounded Dee. Jude grabbed his hair again and twisted.

"*Patieris agonia ob tuus peccata, daemon*" [*You will suffer agony for your sins, demon*], Jude hissed, his gaze darting over Dee's face, taking in his desperate terror.

"*Fortase nos occidere*" [*Perhaps we will kill you*], Lucas murmured, leaning his weight on Dee, bending over him until his lips were almost at his ear. "*Si nos decernimus passus es satis*" [*If we decide you have suffered enough*].

"K-kill me, *please*," Dee gasped. He could feel the bones in his shoulder grinding together – and could feel them already trying to knit, to mend. "Kill me n-now, please, Powers, *mercy* – "

Jude's grip on Dee's hair loosened, his fingers sliding through almost gently. "'Thou therefore, O Lord God of hosts, the God of Israel, awake to visit all the heathen: be not merciful to any wicked transgressors.'" His lips pulled into a devastating smile. "There is no mercy for you or your kind."

Dread stole the pleas from Dee's mouth. He trembled beneath Lucas, muscles straining, pulled tight enough to snap. Tears welled in his eyes as the angels stared down at him, cold and calm and merciless. There was a feverish light in Lucas' eyes that had nothing to do with his heavenly glow. Dee could not fill his lungs with the angel crushing his chest.

He didn't need to. This body was dead, he was only the thing inside it. Despair crawled inside him and settled, comfortable and familiar.

"I think it's time to put this back on," Dominic said softly from outside the circle of harsh light. He stepped forward. His face was cast in stark relief, making him look frightening, inhuman. Monstrous. In his hand he held a broken circle of iron, a

11

hinge connecting the two sides. Dee moaned, his voice breaking, as he stared at the iron collar.

Dominic dropped to one knee beside Lucas. Jude snapped Dee's head back, baring his throat, drawing a broken whine from him. The iron collar closed around his neck. Dominic's hand passed over the collar and when he pulled it away, it was a solid, unbroken band of iron around Dee's neck, with a ring hanging off the front for a chain.

"So begins your second penance, little snake," Lucas purred.

"*N-no*," Dee whimpered. His vision blurred with tears as he lay on the floor, helpless, senseless, the cement leaching heat from his body through his clothes. Tears rolled down his temples and into his hair, smelling faintly of sulfur. The angels only smiled wider as he burned under the collar and cuffs.

3

Tears streamed down Dee's cheeks. His mouth gaped open, his fangs flashing and dripping with his own blood from piercing through his gums. The collar was pulled tight and chained to the ceiling, crushing his throat, choking him. His hands were still cuffed behind him, chained to the floor, keeping him on his knees and fighting desperately for every breath.

He tried to hold his breath, he *tried*, but this body was stronger than he was. This body remembered the feeling of being choked, of needing air, because she had suffered the same tortures he had – for a little while. As Dee struggled and whimpered and choked, the body took over. The body tried to save itself, even as Dee suffered inside it.

He tried to track the angels moving around him in a constant, shifting circle, tried desperately to watch where they were, to prepare for another blow. His vision blurred with tears and panic. The sound of the angels' laughter echoed in his ears until he thought he would be sick with it.

Pain exploded against his back and he screamed, a broken, animal sound that tore his throat as he made it. His vision went white, then black, as he sagged forward, held upright only by the collar that seemed to constrict around his neck. His throat itched and burned, his wrists already blistering from the cuffs digging into his skin. He sobbed and twisted, writhing, desperate.

"Sad little demon," Dominic mocked behind him – Dee could *hear* the angel's knuckles creaking as he gripped the cane. He shuddered and cringed away, mindlessly tugging against the cuffs keeping him chained to the floor. His shoulder exploded in agony.

"Its screams are just as lovely," Lucas murmured, stepping forward into the stark circle of light, pinning Dee with his gaze. Dee went still, whimpering, as Lucas reached out with one hand and gently stroked his thumb along Dee's cheek. Dee shrieked as it singed his skin, the tears sizzling and steaming under the angel's touch. "Better, perhaps. Maybe its jaunt in the world helped it return to us restored, ready for more punishment."

"P-please," Dee breathed, staring up at the angel with wide, terrified eyes. "Please, *potestas*, p – " [*Power*]

Dee gasped as a stinging blow snapped his head to the side.

"I've *told you*, filth," Lucas growled. "That language is *not* for you."

14

Dee's mind was a scattered cacophony of panic. The words were on his tongue, the pleas burning his throat. "*Obse* – P-please, I – I'm *sorry*, Power, please, *mercy, mercy, please* – "

"How *spoiled* you've become, *serpentis*," Lucas murmured, clutching Dee's hair and dragging him forward. The collar closed on his throat. The cuffs tore his wrists and he let out a strangled cry. "You used to know your place. 'Blows and wounds scrub away evil,'" Lucas said with a smile. "'And beatings purge the inmost being.' Did you forget that, little snake, when you were corrupting the little human who took you into their heart?"

Ice clutched at Dee's chest. His desperate, whistling gasps ceased, and his body went rigid. His mouth gaped and gray clouded his vision.

Lucas' smile widened, and his eyes burned into Dee. "Oh," he breathed. "You didn't know we knew about them."

"It's rather amusing," Jude said, stepping closer and standing at Lucas' elbow. "You and the human. Do they think you're human, too? Do they know the vile filth they let into their home?"

"Certainly confusing on the part of the Virtues," Dominic said as he fell in on Lucas' other side. He traced the tip of the cane across Dee's throat, down his chest, then pressed it against his stomach, harder and harder until Dee let out a piteous whine. Lucas' grip on his hair tightened and he dragged him forward harder, pressing the cane deeper into his soft, exposed abdomen, tightening the cuffs and collar even more. Tears streamed down Dee's face and onto the cement floor below as he choked and sobbed.

"They gave us the idea of how to ward ourselves, though," Jude said with a chuckle. "Just draw a sigil that makes the car and house undiscoverable to angels, then pop the house's address in the GPS, and use that to find the house after that." He shrugged. "It's weirdly brilliant. The things these humans can do with their technology ..."

"M-merc-cy – " Dee mouthed. He couldn't draw in air to beg with. He shuddered and weakly tossed his head against the angel's grip.

"After all the things you've done?" Lucas murmured, drawing closer, craning Dee's head back so he was forced to look at him. It relieved a little of the pressure on his throat, and he gasped in a breath. "Oh, little snake." He released Dee's hair all at once. Dee's eyes rolled back as he dragged in breath after desperate breath. "'Ye are of your father the devil, and the lusts of your father ye will do. He was a murderer from the beginning, and abode not in the truth, because there is no truth in him. When he speaketh a lie, he speaketh of his own: for he is a liar, and the father of it.'" He grinned, tilting his head to survey Dee. "There is no mercy for you. You are the enemy, little one. Your words and air and blood are poison. You possessed this body when it was not yours to take. You corrupted the human and manipulated them into being kind to you. Do you believe you deserve salvation, *inimicus*?" [*enemy*]

Dee couldn't speak. He sobbed raggedly and sagged forward, barely able to keep upright. The collar tightened on his throat again.

"Hm," Lucas hummed. Dee raised his head and watched Lucas' smile grow, twisting the corners of his mouth into a devastating grin. "I imagine the human's touch was the first touch you've felt in *years* that didn't burn you, hm, *daemon?*" His hand drifted up, hovering at Dee's cheek. Dee sobbed and twisted away. A warm line of blood rolled down his neck from the torn blisters at his throat.

"This is the only touch you deserve, little monster," Lucas whispered. He grabbed Dee's face in an iron grip and smiled as the demon roared in agony.

4

— · —

Dee shuddered as the angels kicked him again, in the stomach this time. He dragged in a ragged gasp, blinking against the blindfold. Tears had wet through the fabric long ago. He lay on his side now – the angels had finally let him down from the chain dragging him upright, finally unchained his hands from the floor. They stayed locked behind his back. The cement floor sucked the heat from his body where he lay – helpless. Exposed. Open.

His body *hurt,* a terrible throbbing ache that stabbed through his shoulder, crushed his abdomen, burned his back. The bones in his shoulder were still trying to mend. The prickling heat inside him itched, even under the pain.

"*M-mercy,*" he rasped, eyes rolling back against the pain. Blood dripped down his back from the lashes of the cane, soaking into his shirt and trickling onto the floor.

Ilya gave me this shirt.

"Mercy," he croaked. "Mercy, *mer* – " He was cut off by a scream as the angels kicked his broken shoulder. His vision went

18

even blacker behind the blindfold and a ringing started in his ears. He convulsed and gagged. Nothing came up. There was nothing in his stomach anymore. Dee's head spun.

Jude spoke. "'He shall smite the earth, and with the breath of his lips shall he slay the wicked.'"

Dee jerked away from a kick to his ribs. Something *snapped* inside him. Agony clutched his chest, sharpened when Dee screamed. Sweat beaded on his forehead. His mouth gaped open and he sucked in a shallow breath, desperate.

"K-kill – *please* – kill me, I beg you, merciful Powers, please, I beg – "

He let out a twisted wail as he was forced onto his back. His hands were crushed beneath him as an angel straddled his hips and pinned him down by his throat. His skin blistered under the angel's hands. He tipped his head back against the cold floor and shrieked his agony.

Then, mercifully, the hands disappeared. Dee coughed, sucking in breath after panicked breath. His broken rib creaked inside him, sending stabbing pain through his chest, up his neck, down his arm –

His lung burned too. Dee dragged in another breath and cried out as the pain pierced him again, as real as any knife. He shuddered and went still.

They've punctured my lung.

He heaved a ragged sob. He writhed under the angel, desperate to relieve the press of the cement against the shifting bones

19

in his chest and shoulder. He sucked in another lungful of air, let it out.

He knew this body and its pain well enough to know there was air leaking into his chest through the tear in his lung.

I don't need to breathe.

Tears dripped from the soaked blindfold and into his hair. He shivered and forced his chest to be still. Desperately, he tried to focus his energy on repairing the lung, the rib. His shoulder flared again with pain. He was sick with it.

A rough cloth settled around his neck and he tilted his head, desperate to understand what was going on. Heavy hands pressed down over the cloth a moment later, constricting his bruised and blistered throat. His mouth opened and he fought for air – an instinct. His eyes rolled back behind the blindfold and he twitched under the angel's weight.

"That's better. Don't want to burn through to your trachea *just* yet," Lucas purred, his voice sounding like it was only inches above Dee. "Mmmn. There's nothing quite like watching a vile monster fight for air."

Dee couldn't make a sound. He thrashed weakly, eyes wide with terror beneath the blindfold. He waited for his hearing to fade, for the embrace of darkness to save him from the pain. It didn't come. He knew it wouldn't.

His heart no longer pumped blood anymore. His cells no longer needed it. He would be awake – and alive – until the angels slid their knives of consecrated iron between his ribs.

He'd begged Ilya to do it. Fever-drunk and delirious, he'd looked up at them from his sickbed and *begged*.

Ilya would have been kinder.

Something tore in Dee's shoulder as he yanked against the cuffs locking his hands behind his back. He kicked his feet against the floor, shoes squeaking on the cement, wild with panic.

"Beautiful," Jude breathed from somewhere above Dee. A shoe nudged his ribs. He jerked, his mouth pulled open in a silent scream.

Lucas chuckled and, for a brief moment, loosened his hands around Dee's neck. Dee dragged in a tortured breath, the air whistling through his throat, before he convulsed in a fit of coughing. Then Lucas pressed down again, cutting off his air.

"What a silly *daemon*," Lucas crooned. His breath fanned out over Dee's face. "You truly believed you were safe, didn't you?"

I hoped –

"How astronomically foolish you are, little one," Lucas murmured. "You really believed that the human could find it even in their tender heart to feel for you? You really thought an angel of the Lord, a *Virtue*, could care whether you breathed or died?"

A broken, high-pitched sound punched from Dee's throat as a boot collided with his side. Every cell in his body screamed for relief.

21

Lucas' voice darkened, the words said softly before now spewed from gritted teeth. "You are *inimicus*. You are *daemon*. You are *adversator*. You are the Enemy who walks among us. You take what is not given to you. You burn everything you touch."

Tears rolled down Dee's face behind the blindfold. *I know. I know.*

"You are deluded beyond measure, little snake, to have believed you had a place with the humans. If they knew you for what you were, they would cast you out. They would tie you to the stake and burn you alive. They would drown you in holy water – just as we are going to do to you." Lucas' hands tightened around Dee's throat. Stars burst behind his eyes.

An angel's boot settled on his cheek, turning his head to the side. He gagged weakly at how it shifted his throat beneath Lucas' hands.

"This is what you deserve, little snake," Dominic said above him. "To be ground beneath the foot of those who will destroy you, and to suffer under our hands. You were not made for softness. You were not made for human love. You were made to *break*." The boot lifted from Dee's face.

Dee flinched back as best he could, bracing for the kick. *I know all that. I only thought ... I only hoped ...*

"Look how it struggles," Jude whispered. "Look at how it fights. *Lovely.*"

"Mmm," Lucas assented. "So *wicked.*" He chuckled softly, leaning harder against Dee's throat. Dee twitched and writhed, mouth open wide as he fought – desperately, fruitlessly – for air. His lungs felt like fire inside him. The moment stretched on, eternal, inescapable.

There was a shift of boots on the floor at Dee's head. "Move, Lucas," Dominic said in the darkness above him, a smile in his voice. "My turn. And take the towel away. I want to watch it *burn.*"

5

Ilya's stomach lurched. Worry burned hot under their skin. Their feet pounded against the sidewalk as they rushed through the park, casting their gaze this way and that, searching desperately. Searching for their demon – their *friend*.

He'd been *right here*.

He'd stopped for some water – and Ilya had been so proud of him, so grateful that he felt safe enough in their presence to want water and *take* it, without begging, without terror. They had turned away from the drinking fountain for the briefest moment, raising their gaze to the shimmering crown of leaves at the tops of the trees, rippling in the cool wind. They had opened their mouth to say to Dee, *look at that. Isn't that beautiful?*

Then they'd turned back, and he was gone.

Gone.

Ilya's heart clenched. He couldn't have gone *far*, he ... he wouldn't have just ... *left*. He wouldn't have left them. He wouldn't have just disappeared.

Then where is *he?*

Their mouth was dry as they reached for the phone in their pocket. Dee didn't have one on him, so Ilya wouldn't be able to call. He'd never wanted a phone. He was content to stay by their side whenever he could gather the strength to leave the house, staying close to Ilya or Dara or Evangeline. Even if being near the angels still made him tremble.

Ilya's heart leapt as they turned and smacked right into Dara, where moments before there had only been empty air.

"Where is he?" she murmured, golden eyes blazing.

Ilya blanched and fell back a step. Protective anger rose in their throat. "H-he didn't ... he didn't do anything, Dara, I just can't find – "

"No," Dara huffed, lifting her head as if trying to hear a faraway voice. "*Where is he*?"

Ilya shuddered and turned to survey the park again. "What do you mean?" they murmured. Their fingertips began to tingle. "Wh-why are you ... What happened?"

"He's ... he suddenly got very scared," she whispered.

Ilya's heart sank in their chest. "What?" they breathed. Their hand drifted out to take hers. Her fingers were cool and dry.

"He was out with you, right?" Dara said, still peering around the park, the air around her starting to vibrate. "You were out for a walk?"

"Yeah," Ilya said, their voice shaking. "Yeah. Just a ... a walk. He was doing so well and then I turned around and he was ... was gone."

"How long ago?" Dara mumbled. Her hand seemed to grow colder in theirs, seemed to suck the heat right from their body.

"Um ..." Ilya blinked against the tears that were clouding their vision. "Um ... A minute or two ago?"

Dara let out a breath. The smell of ozone washed over Ilya. They tugged at Dara's hand, desperately trying to duck into her line of sight. "What happened?" they whimpered, and couldn't hold back a full-body shiver. "Dara ... what is it?"

A muscle ticked in Dara's jaw, and she pinned Ilya with her gaze. The world seemed frozen around them, the breath of the breeze and the thud of Ilya's heart against their ribs and the movement of the sun in the sky all seeming to cease for a long moment. Dara wet her lips and looked away. Ilya heaved a sigh of meager relief.

"A minute or so ago," Dara murmured, her voice pitched low and rippling through the ground around them, "Dee suddenly felt ... frightened. It was like ... he cried out, and I could hear him ... all the way across town. I f-felt his, um, his pain, and ... and his terror."

"H-how is that even possible?" Ilya breathed.

"I feel this with both of you," Dara said, waving away the question. "So I can make sure you're safe. But I ... What I felt is, um ..." Slowly, her gaze slid across the grass and the trees around them and settled on the drinking fountain Dee had paused at only minutes before. She lurched toward it, and somehow even that motion was unfathomably graceful. Ilya stumbled along behind.

Dara stopped in front of the drinking fountain and reached out to touch it, letting her fingers brush the shiny chrome. Her eyes slid closed, and the very air around Ilya began to hum. Then, with a punch through Ilya's chest like a bolt of lightning, her eyes flew open and she gripped the handle.

"***Lucas***," she hissed through her teeth.

Ilya staggered back and slammed their hands over their ears as the word seemed to tear the air apart. They could not block out the sound that crashed over them, sounding like continents being smashed to pieces, like the sky cracking open above them. All around them, people turned their heads instinctively toward the sound, even though Ilya knew they could not see Dara.

Not if she didn't want them to.

"Wh-who is Lucas?" Ilya whimpered, trembling from head to toe in the wake of the angel's wrath, pulling their shaking hands away from their ears.

"The one who took him before," Dara snarled. "The Power. It was him, Dominic, and Jude ... Those are the ... the ones who – who *took* Dee before, and – "

Ilya couldn't hold back a sob. "A-and they took him again? Are you ..." They blinked. Tears spilled down their cheeks. "Are you *sure*?" they breathed.

"I'm sure," Dara said, the air still buzzing around her, but settling, cooling.

"*Why*?" Ilya whimpered. They raised their gaze to Dara's, terrified of what they would find there. When they read the confirmation in her eyes – the rage, the *sorrow* – they crumpled, anguished.

"W-we have to *find* him," they sobbed. "They'll – they'll hurt him, Dara, please, I can't let him ... We have to *save him*." They gasped and clutched at Dara's hand. "Can you feel him? Like you did before? Can you feel him right now? Please, Dara, *please* ..."

Dara's eyes fell shut, and she drew in a deep breath. It was like the very air around Ilya was breathing. When she let it out, they felt ice pierce the air around them. She opened her eyes. When she raised them to Ilya's, they were pained. Ilya whimpered and pressed a hand to their mouth.

"He's ... in pain," Dara whispered.

"*No*," Ilya sobbed. "*No*. N-not again." Dara's hand tightened in theirs. They dashed the tears from their eyes. "Where? Can you ... c-can you feel where? You found him before – "

"No," Dara murmured, her eyes unfocused. "I can't ... They're using ..." She paled. The sun shimmered on her skin. "They're using the rune that *we* use to conceal the house. They're ... they're taking him ..." Her throat bobbed. "I can't *find* him."

"H-how did you find him before?" Ilya said, trembling. "When they were ... were hurting him."

"By *accident*," Dara said. Her voice sounded fragile – not like glass, but like a bomb. "We were in the area for a meeting with another fucking garrison and heard him, um ... screaming."

Ilya pressed their hands against their mouth and heaved another sob. "No. *No.* H-he's taken so m-much pain, *no* ... Dara, we, please, we have to ... Dara, what do I *do*?"

"I don't know," Dara murmured. When she looked up to the sky, she seemed to glow with a ferocious light all her own. Her eyes flashed and her lip curled. "We're going to find him. We're going to *find* him."

6

Dee lay at the angels' feet, senseless and shuddering. He was curled on his side with his hands still cuffed behind him. He felt the crushing burn of the bones in his shoulder trying to mend, his muscles trying to pull them back into place so they could fuse and solidify. He gasped weakly against the pain as it spiked and faded and spiked again in his body. He'd given up on not breathing long ago – he didn't have the strength to hold his breath. Still, he could feel the pressure of his lung collapsing slowly, like a fist squeezing his heart. The pain hollowed him out and shattered him under its weight.

A tight band of burned flesh wound around his neck in the perfect shape of Dominic's hand. His cheeks were singed, too, where Lucas had grabbed him. And on his back, long, bloody slashes from the cane stung and ached with each breath. The raw skin around his wrists and throat felt distant and dull compared to the other hurts in his body. But at least they'd given him his air again.

They'd given him back his sight, too. His eyes streamed tears that dripped onto the cement floor beneath him. He watched the angels as they moved around him in the shadows beyond the stark circle of light on the floor, laughing, murmuring, making plans. Plans for Dee's pain, and for his penance.

He could no longer listen. He would suffer it all eventually. After so long in their captivity before – *years, it had to be years, Lucas mentioned years* – he knew there were no limits to the angels' cruelty. Chained, collared, broken, *alone* – he would suffer, and break even more. There was no mercy in the angels' eyes. Mercy would never find him again. Not with the warding symbol on the door.

Ilya was merciful. Ilya was kind.

Dee could barely remember their gentle touch. All he could feel was his body burning around him.

His silent heart plunged in his chest as the angels stepped forward into the light surrounding him. He whined, an animal sound, and pressed his face against the floor. He waited, perfectly still, for the blow to fall, for the burning hands to grab him, for the knife to carve into his flesh. He shivered, and waited. And waited.

Finally, when he could not wait any longer, he raised his gaze to the angels, shaking so hard his teeth chattered. He couldn't suppress a moan of agony as the bones shifted in his shoulder.

Still, they were mending. They were mending.

He lay helpless and bound under the angels' deadly stares. His terror was a shard of ice that burrowed deeper and deeper inside him.

Lucas grinned and wet his lips. "**Beg**," he commanded, and the word was a bolt of thunder in Dee's ears.

Dee would not have needed the command. He opened his mouth and sobbed, *"Please."*

The angels chuckled in the circle around him. "**Again**," Lucas said, the word shaking the very foundation of the house.

Dee groaned as the sound crushed him against the floor. He cowered away from the angels, drawing his knees up to his chest and clenching his hands into fists behind his back. "P-please, *please*, angels, Powers, m-mercy, please, *please*, d-don't hurt me …" His lips were numb. He thought he might be sick.

"It used to be better at begging, I think," Jude said, tilting his head as he stared at Dee. He took a heavy step forward and crouched at Dee's side.

"*N-no!*" Dee shrieked, his feet scrabbling against the floor as he tried to twist away. "*Obsecro, potestates –* "

He gasped as a blow snapped his head to the side, cracking it on the cold cement floor. The coppery taste of his own blood burst across his tongue. He sobbed weakly as blood dripped from his lips.

"F-forgive me, angels," Dee whimpered, his head spinning. "H-have mercy on m-me, please, *please, mercy, please, please, please …*"

"It's spoiled," Dominic said with a grin. "Living in that house for so long, allowed to walk freely instead of being forced to its knees, allowed to sleep in a bed and eat from a table ..." He snorted and tossed his head in a peal of laughter. "Instead of putting it in iron chains and *breaking* it like the monster it is ..."

Lucas stepped forward and nudged Dee's chin up with the toe of his boot. Dee fell still and looked up at the angel, trembling, lips still moving in a silent prayer for mercy. Lucas' grin spread wider across his face, lips pulling back to show his teeth. Dee shivered, powerless to look away.

"Beg for water, little snake," Lucas rumbled.

"P-please." The word was torn from Dee's lips, even as he began to cry harder, shaking his head in desperation. He could already feel the holy water pouring down his throat, could already feel the inescapable agony as it burned him all the way down, poisoning him, devouring him from the inside out. "P-please, angels, w-water, water ... N-no, *please* – "

"All you had to do was ask," Jude murmured. He reached down and drew one finger down Dee's cheek. Dee writhed and sobbed under the touch.

Lucas knelt, his hand darting out and fisting in Dee's hair. He jerked Dee's head to the side, forcing him onto his back again. The angels laughed as Lucas held a bottle over Dee's head, the lid off, the water filling it and trembling at the brim.

"Powers, please, *no*!" Dee screamed, trying desperately to turn his head away.

"Our little sinner has asked for water," Lucas said. He forced Dee's head back, baring his throat. "And it has asked for mercy. Of course, we'll oblige."

Dee screamed in anguish as Lucas poured the holy water over his face, immediately blistering his skin. Then Jude forced his jaw open with a burning hand, and Dee was drowning in fire.

7

— • —

Dee's screams shattered in his own ears. With his arms stretched up above him and cuffed to the ceiling, and his feet barely able to reach the floor, he could hardly draw a full breath. His feet and calves burned, shaking under his weight as he strained to balance on the tips of his toes. His breaths came in shallow, anguished pants, his lung slowly collapsing with each gulping inhale. His shoulder was a blaze of agony, fractured ends of bone grinding together as he tried – and failed – to hold perfectly still through the beating.

The angels stood around him in a semi-circle, their smiles wide and their eyes flashing, merciless and cold. Dee shuddered and turned desperate eyes on them, tears stinging his cheeks and tasting bitter on his tongue.

"P-please," he whispered, his voice broken, his throat raw and blistered from the holy water. "Please, merciful Powers. K-kill me."

Dominic smirked. He stepped forward and reached out to stabilize Dee with a hand on his shoulder, fisting in the cloth of his shirt. Dee sobbed and squeezed his eyes shut, just before the blow smashed into his abdomen.

He let out a rasping scream as white exploded behind his eyes. Pain crashed through his shoulder, through his stomach, through his throat, building and building until he thought he would die from it. He tilted his head back and wailed his agony, eyes fixed sightlessly on the ceiling. Ice seemed to pierce him down to his bones. His blood cooled on his back from the cane marks that had been torn open again from his struggles.

"We *are* merciful, aren't we?" Jude crooned as he stepped forward, reaching out and smoothing his fingers through Dee's sweaty, tangled hair. Dee whimpered as the smell of burning hair made him gag. "We could have done what they did in the old days. Flayed the skin from your body, hanged you and left you there for days and days, burned you in the fires so like the ones we may eventually return you to ..." He smiled. There was no kindness in his eyes, no grace. He leaned in closer, twisted his hand in Dee's hair until Dee whimpered.

"You know, Lucas," Jude murmured, his gaze moving over Dee, taking in his terror, his pain. "I really would like to kill this one eventually."

Lucas cocked an eyebrow. "Oh?"

"Yes," Jude said softly. His breath felt like ice on Dee's skin. "It's fun to play with, and we are doing our Lord's work in overseeing its penance, but ..." His lips curved up, and Dee squirmed under his gaze. "I want to watch the fire leave its eyes.

I want to watch it die, knowing we have done good work in purging it from this earth."

Dee's eyes fell shut, sending tears coursing down his cheeks. "*P-please,*" he breathed.

"Just ... not for a while, right?" Dominic said, petulant.

"Oh, no," Jude said with a chuckle. "No, I think we could still get a few good years out of this one."

Dee whimpered. "N-no – "

His head snapped to the side as Jude struck him across the face. A warm trickle of blood spilled from Dee's mouth and down his chin as he slumped, limp in his shackles. Pain burst through his shoulder and he cried out, scrambling to get his feet back underneath him.

"Hm." Jude nudged Dee's chin up and smiled when Dee's skin sizzled under the touch. Dee turned his head and pressed his face against his arm, sobbing, helpless. "Yes, perhaps a few good years, but then ..." Jude leaned in closer, so close that Dee could see the flat gold of his eyes. "I'm going to slide my knife of consecrated iron into your heart – and look in your eyes as I send you to burn in Hell, little one."

Dee's parched and aching throat tightened as he cowered away from the inhuman loathing in Jude's eyes. If they killed him with their consecrated blades, there would be no Hell waiting for him. Not without a human soul to tether himself to as he fell. He would simply cease to exist, would simply disappear into nothingness. No soul, no spirit, no piece of him would remain. If they killed him in this body, he would be gone forever.

He squeezed his eyes shut and cried out as Ilya leapt to his thoughts, *his* Ilya, kind and trusting and true. His Ilya, the one who held him, loved him, cradled him gently when he was sick and scared and hurting, when he was shaking from memories of the torture he'd endured at the hands of angels.

These angels.

He opened his eyes and raised them, once again, to Jude.

Do it now. Please, please, do it now.

Jude wound up and whipped a vicious backhand across Dee's face. He gasped, stunned, his head spinning from the blow. More blood streamed down his chin, staining his shirt. He coughed. Red spattered Jude's face. Dee moaned in terror as Jude froze with his hand pulled back for another strike.

Slowly, slowly, Jude reached up and wiped his face with his sleeve. Dee couldn't breathe; terror squeezed his heart like a vice. His throat closed. His legs threatened to give out, sparking fire and agony in his shoulder.

"Maybe we could use a break to clean up," Lucas said light-heartedly.

Jude huffed. "Indeed. I'm sullied, now." He swiped at his face again, leaving garish streaks of blood on his cheek. "Although I should have expected to get filthy while battling the scum of the earth ... Still." He paused, hovering between taking a step forward and taking a step back, his gaze fixed on Dee.

Lucas sauntered to the steps and climbed the first one. "It's almost time for our report to Ezekiel, anyway."

Jude was still staring at Dee, his eyes lingering on the smear of blood on Dee's lips. "I somehow thought its blood would burn me, or something."

"Enough of it will," Lucas said with a shrug. "If it's from a stronger demon. With this one, its blood is barely stronger than water. It's not even corporeal."

"Interesting," Jude mused. He stepped away. Dee let out a piteous sob of relief.

Dominic snapped his fingers. The chains released from the ceiling and Dee toppled to the floor, unable to slow his fall. His mouth stretched open in a silent scream as his shoulder crunched with the impact. He lay shuddering on the icy floor, shackled and bleeding. His broken rib grated with each breath. He groaned and rolled onto his other side, doing his best to cradle his shoulder. He shuddered as pain broke over him, again and again and again.

Lucas paused on the steps. "It's wearing out so *quickly*," he said with a scoff.

"We've been more enthusiastic this time," Dominic said, a hint of a laugh in his voice.

"Hm. True. And it's just … healing slower." Lucas tilted his head. His eyes flashed and his teeth showed in a grin. "We're going to be back in an hour," he said, pinning Dee with his gaze. "So until then … **heal, demon**."

Dee writhed, back arching, as the command gripped him. Every bit of his body cried out at once, demanding his energy, desperate for relief. The grating itch of mending bones crescendoed into a blaze of heat. His blood burned in his veins as the angels turned and, laughing, left him alone in the stark circle of light, lying crumpled in a heap on the cold basement floor.

8

— · —

Dee's throat could only manage a croaking whisper as he burned. The bones in his shoulder blazed like fire under his skin. His muscles juddered and shook, straining to hold the bones in place as they mended – taking minutes, when before it had always taken days. The charred flesh all over his body went raw and bloody, softening, stinging, as new skin grew to cover it. The cane marks on his back broke open again, weeping blood before they sealed, leaving only a shadow of pale skin where each mark had been.

The room spun around him in a dizzy-sick kaleidoscope of agony. The scent of his own blood was thick and bitter in his nostrils, metallic and smelling faintly of sulfur. He could not tell if his eyes were open or closed; all he saw was white, a stab of cold light piercing into him, swallowing him whole.

And through it all, Dee could only lie helpless on the floor and scream – or try to. His throat was still blistered from the water. Or perhaps torn from the screaming.

With each agonized breath, he felt the air in his chest thin, his lung inflating again, throbbing and aching from being crushed. He drew in bigger and bigger lungfuls of air that he didn't need. He kept drawing breaths he didn't need.

He kept drawing breaths he didn't *deserve.*

He shuddered and sobbed weakly. The collar felt familiar around his neck, more familiar than freedom had ever been. He felt its weight and its sting, felt how it rubbed his skin to raw, then bleeding. He felt how it had imprinted in his skin when he'd been strung up from it. He felt how it seemed almost *molded* to him, fitting his throat with only a finger's-breadth of space around it. He smelled the sour tang of the metal against his skin, mixing with the smell of his blood and sweat. He wondered if, since his blood was poison to all things holy, it would eat through the iron, with time.

That hadn't happened in the years he'd spent under Lucas' boot, Dominic's fists, or Jude's scalding touch. Perhaps if the Virtues never came for him, he would be here until the building crumbled around him, until the iron rusted away into dust.

He wished, dizzily, that he could meet such a simple end.

Perhaps that's how it would be. Perhaps when they finally slid their blades into him he would simply rust away, all the scattered stardust pieces of this body disintegrating into dust and blowing away, to become motes floating on a sunbeam, to become the imperfection in a drop of rain. He moaned weakly and twisted against the floor, shivering as his fangs descended with the next flash of agony. Even so, he was grateful to the Powers. They had commanded him to be healed. He could feel the fresh, pink skin blooming on his cheeks and throat, and shivered. His shoulder would take more time, but it was healing. He was healing.

He was *mending*. And with every repair, the body sucked away more of his energy, more of his strength. But slowly, steadily, the pain was fading, even under the initial agony of the command.

Thus saith the Lord, the God of David thy father, I have heard thy prayer, I have seen thy tears: behold, I will heal thee.

Dee shuddered and let out a plaintive moan. *That's not for me; that's for them. I'm a monster. I'm the one who possessed an innocent human and corrupted another one ...*

But he had just wanted to *feel* something. He just wanted to experience the things he'd only heard described in hushed, reverent tones by the other demons he'd known in Hell. He only wanted to experience the colors and sounds, the music, the lush textures of fabric on his body and food in his mouth, the press of another human against him, dancing, hugging, laughing, lips on cheeks and hands on hearts – he'd just wanted to *feel* it, something good and rich, something he'd heard so much about but could never have imagined.

He'd only been *borrowing* the body. He was always going to give it back.

And now the woman was dead, and he prayed with every fiber of her stolen body that she was at peace. As for him, he would burn, and he would deserve it.

His hands balled into fists and he sobbed as his shoulder gave a particularly painful wrench. His voice was louder now, stronger. When he swallowed, it didn't feel like swallowing a knife.

Surely the angels wouldn't allow him to live with such relief for long. Surely the angels would want to tear him open again and revel in his screams and pleas.

As if he had summoned them with his thoughts, the door to the basement opened. Dee let out a piteous wail. His burns were healed, but his shoulder was still crushed with agony. The bones weren't fused yet. They shifted and creaked when he lifted his head to look at the angels as they descended the steps one by one, their unearthly gazes fixed on him.

When Lucas reached the basement floor, his lips quirked into a smile. "We've just had the *best* idea," he said. Dee sobbed when the others began to laugh.

9

—·—

"*N-no*," Dee sobbed as the angels stepped toward him. His shoes squeaked against the floor as he tried to drag himself away with his hands still locked behind him, agony rising and breaking through his shoulder. He felt the edges of the Trap like the hum of an electric fence. Sweat broke out over his newly-healed skin. "P-please, *no* ..."

"It looks *much* better," Lucas said with the hint of a pout in his voice. "I didn't think it would work so fast." He cleared his throat. "**Demon, stop healing**."

Dee's mouth fell open and he wailed against the floor. All at once, he could feel the bones in his shoulder stop knitting together. He could feel every healing fiber of his body stop. Not even the slow creep of his own mending continued. The iron blistered his skin, and it did not begin to mend again. His tears stung his cheeks as he sobbed.

A vicious hand closed on his hair and dragged him back into the center of the Trap. He gasped as he was thrown to the floor again. His head cracked against the cement floor.

"P-please," he heaved, turning his head to look up at the angels standing around him. "Please, *please*, Powers, y-you have stopped all my healing, I c-cannot – "

He cried out as Dominic kicked him hard in the chest. He realized, distantly, that his lung was restored, the rib still fractured but no longer piercing into him now. Through the ringing in his ears, he could barely hear the angels speaking above him. He whimpered and gasped – grateful, at least, for his air. For as long as he had it.

He froze when the angels stopped murmuring above him and turned to look down on him once again. Jude knelt down beside him and reached out to run a hand through his hair. He shuddered under the touch that he could feel singeing his hair.

"We'll let you heal later, little one," Jude crooned. "Can't have you wearing out too quickly. Remember, we'll want to keep you for *years*." He smiled when Dee whimpered softly. "But you don't need to heal for this part." He chuckled and glanced up at Dominic. "Ready?"

"Yes," Dominic said with a grin as he knelt beside Jude. Dee blinked away tears, and they ran down his cheeks. His gaze found Dominic again – and every muscle in his body went rigid.

Dominic was holding a knife.

The edge glittered under the yellowed light, impossibly sharp, seeming to cut the very air – and seeming almost to have a light all its own. Dee's heart ached as he stared at the blade of consecrated iron, held inches from his face. Then he nodded silently and rolled onto his back, tilting his head to bare his throat to them.

But Ilya …

Tears burned in his eyes and he convulsed with a sob. *Ilya, Ilya, Ilya, my Ilya … Custodire eos, Deus, benedicere eos, custodire eos a malum sicut me …* [*Ilya, Ilya, Ilya, my Ilya … Protect them, God, bless them, protect them from evil like me …*]

"Oh, little snake," Lucas said, kneeling beside his head. "Haven't you been listening?"

Cold gripped Dee's chest.

"We're not going to kill you," Jude said gently, his lips curved in a mockery of a smile. "Not for many years. Not until you have *truly* paid for your sins – and oh, little sinner, they are *many*."

Dee looked up at them in terror, eyes flicking between each angel, and then finally back to the knife that glinted in Dominic's hand. He wet his lips and shuddered as more tears coursed down his temples and into his hair.

Dominic smirked as he bent over Dee. "Still, this position is perfect." He grabbed the ring of Dee's iron collar, holding him in place – then brought the knife to Dee's throat and made a cut over where his pulse once beat.

Dee sobbed in panic as the blood spilled out over his throat and pooled on the floor beneath him. He didn't need his blood – he didn't, he could live without it – but his body rebelled, and he writhed against the heavy hand pinning him down by his collar. He dragged in breath after desperate breath as tears blurred his vision and spilled down his temples.

Above him, Dominic held the knife to the palm of his own hand – and cut. When he pressed his hand to the wound, Dee *screamed.*

Dominic's blood spilled out over Dee's throat, leaving blistering skin in its wake. It seeped inside the cut and pooled in Dee's veins, burning him from the inside out. Dee's shoulder tore as he thrashed against the cuffs, mindless, fangs breaking through and flashing as his mouth opened wide with his scream. He sounded like an animal in a trap, like a creature being torn to pieces.

Above him, Dominic frowned. "It's not ... spreading."

Lucas tilted his head. "Has it always not had a heartbeat?" He stared down at Dee as he burned. **"Demon, make your heart beat, spread the blood through your body."**

Inside Dee's chest, his heart shuddered, then contracted in a single, sluggish beat. Then, again. And again. Every beat felt like a knife going through him, a spasm of pain. As his heart beat, the angel's blood spread slowly – and lit every nerve on fire in its wake.

Dee threw his head back and roared with agony. A line of fire moved from the wound at his throat, down inside him to his chest – and then everywhere else. Every lethargic pump of his dead heart spread the poison to every vessel, every cell. Another beat, then another. Dee convulsed as it spread, barely feeling the flash of pain as Dominic pressed his finger to the cut at Dee's throat, cauterizing it shut, keeping the angel's blood trapped inside him.

Dee's heart beat once more, then fell silent again in his chest. Dee was burning alive.

Lucas peered down at Dee, his eyes fixed on him as he sobbed and twisted against the floor. "'For the life of the flesh is in the blood: and I have given it to you upon the altar to make an atonement for your souls: for it is the blood that maketh an atonement for the soul.' This is righteous justice, little one, for your profane existence. Be grateful that we are punishing you for your sins." His hand tightened in Dee's hair and he jerked his head back, smiling at how Dee's pupils were blown wide with agony, his fangs flashing in the light as he jerked and screamed. "Be *grateful*, little sinner," he murmured.

"*B-bene facis*" [*Th-thank you*], Dee heaved. He gasped as Lucas whipped a hand across his face so hard that he pitched onto his side. He arched back, mouth open wide with his desperate shrieks. "Th-thank you, m-merciful ... Ahh, *please, please, please, no* – "

His eyes rolled back and he retched. Acid burned his throat like holy water. He convulsed as fire burned through his veins, consuming him, tearing him apart from the inside out. Sweat poured down his skin, soaking his clothes and hair. He left smears on the floor as he tried to twist away from the pain that had burrowed deep inside him.

"Told you this was a good idea," Dominic said somewhere above Dee.

Dee opened his eyes and saw the angels standing around him in a circle now, staring down at him as he twitched and sobbed. Fire consumed every part of him. His throat was raw from screaming.

"It won't kill it ... right?" Lucas said, and nudged Dee with his toe. Dee wailed and cringed into himself. His chest heaved with desperate sobs.

"Probably not. I mean ... I don't think anyone's ever ... done this before." Dominic grinned. "But look at it."

Dee's eyes were unfocused as the angels smiled down at him. He choked on a sob and tried to twist away.

"Still, if we want to keep it alive ..." Lucas tilted his head to survey Dee, eyes sweeping him up and down. "**Demon, you may heal at the rate you normally do**." The ground shook under Dee as the command gripped him.

He shuddered as his body rebelled against the poison inside him. He retched again, bringing up nothing but bile. White light flashed across his vision and he hoped, desperately, that he would lose consciousness and slide into the mercy of oblivion. Instead, he felt his body writhe against the floor, desperate to escape the pain and unable to. Then, as if his body had given up entirely on purging the poison from his veins, he felt his shoulder slowly begin to mend again.

He could barely see through the agony as even his eyes burned. He could taste his own blood as he bit his tongue in his panic, fangs piercing deep.

Jude's voice was husky and low. "'Because I have purged thee, and thou wast not purged, thou shalt not be purged from thy filthiness any more, till I have caused my fury to rest upon thee.'" He licked his lips. "Look at the agony in its eyes. *Lovely.*"

Dominic twirled the knife in his hand. His palm was healed, spotless, as if there had never been a wound. "This was an *excellent* idea, if I do say so myself." He grinned at Dee.

Dee shuddered and realized that, slowly, slowly, the fire inside him was fading. He sobbed in meager relief.

"Still," Dominic said as he knelt by Dee's side again. "I forgot how good it felt to have my knife to the little sinner's throat." He pushed Dee onto his back, placed a hand on his chest, and *leaned*. Dee's rib creaked under the weight. He shivered and looked up at Dominic, panting and desperate.

Dominic pressed the tip of the knife to the base of Dee's throat, just barely brushing his skin. Dee squeezed his eyes shut and sobbed weakly.

"Beg," Dominic said, and grinned when the other two laughed. "Beg, little *daemon,* for mercy."

10

— · —

"*P-please*," Dee begged, his throat bobbing with panic. The tip of the knife brushed his skin and instantly cut, sharper than any razor. "P-please, angels ... mercy, please, show me mercy, *please* ..."

Dominic laughed as he straddled Dee's hips and drew the tip of his knife across Dee's throat, light as a feather, above and below the collar in gentle stripes. Dee gasped and sobbed as his skin tingled under the blade. His hands were crushed beneath him, the iron cuffs cutting deep into his wrists. He swallowed, again and again, doing his best to hold still as the angel's blood still burned him from the inside out.

If he just leaned forward ... if he just lifted his head and let the blade cut through his throat ...

My throat or my heart. Please, please, mercy, cut my throat or pierce my heart, please ...

Dominic chuckled as he drew the knife down, over Dee's heaving chest, lower still until the tip rested against his abdomen. Dee quivered, tears streaming into his hair, as Dominic stared down at him with gleeful hatred in his eyes.

"Alright," Dominic said softly. "You've begged. Now. **Confess**."

Dee arched back, his mouth bobbing open as the command gripped him. His lips felt too numb to speak. Every inch of him burned, and his mind was blank with panic. "I-I ..."

"Confess your sins," Jude said gently. He knelt beside Dee's head and wound burning fingers through his hair. Entire hanks of it had been burned away, leaving smoldering ends and bald skin. Jude smiled as he ran a lock of it through his fingers. It singed and curled away, sending wisps of acrid smoke floating up toward the ceiling. "Confess, demon. You were lost to us once, only to be found to be broken anew. Tell us of your evil deeds and we will bring absolution: by purging you from this earth, and your deeds with you."

Dee opened his mouth to speak. His eyes rolled back at the fire in his veins, twisting inside him and breaking him to pieces. He dry-heaved, desperately turning his head so he wouldn't choke. He cried out as the motion jostled the bones in his shoulder.

He screamed as Lucas kicked him hard in his broken shoulder. The newly-healed bones broke apart again, and Dee sobbed in despair. He shuddered as agony swept through him, again and again and again.

"Confess, *daemon*," Lucas spat. "Tell us what you have done."

"*H-habeo –* " [*I h-have*] Dee whined as the knife pressed against his abdomen, easily parting the fabric of his shirt and piercing into the first layer of skin.

"*Nolo dice quod lingua iterum*" [*Do not speak that language again*], Dominic growled above him. "*Tu es indignus dicere eam*" [*You are unworthy to speak it*].

"*S-set est lingua mea*" [*B-but it's my native tongue*], Dee sobbed. "*E-est –* " [*I-it's –*]

A slap rocked his head to the side. "*Nolo. Dice. Quod. Lingua. Dice eam iterum, ero scalpere lingua tua*" [*Do. Not. Speak. That. Language. If you speak it again, I will cut out your tongue*].

Dee sobbed weakly. "Forgive me," he rasped. "Forgive me."

"Confess your sins, and we may just be merciful," Dominic said with a smile.

Dee stared up at him, trembling with hope that he knew he shouldn't have. He wet his lips and was grateful, so grateful, that his mouth had healed from the holy water. His throat was almost too tight to speak.

"I-I ..." he croaked. "I s-stole this body when it was not mine to take."

"Yes, you did," Dominic said with a grin, and slid his knife into Dee's belly.

Dee threw his head back and shrieked his agony as the knife pierced him. He felt the sharp blade bury deep inside, cold and merciless against the unending burn of the angel's blood. Tears pooled in the shells of his ears and streamed onto the concrete floor. Dee writhed under Dominic's weight, his shoes scrabbling for purchase on the floor. He shuddered as Dominic drew out his blade and passed one finger over the wound, sealing it shut.

Dominic held the knife above Dee, glinting with his blood. It dripped onto his shirt – *Ilya's shirt* – staining the cotton bright red. Dee stared at the knife in horror as Dominic turned it back and forth as if inspecting it.

"Good," Dominic said with a smile. "What else?"

"N-no," Dee heaved. He could feel the blood pooling inside him, and could feel the veins and tissues sealing shut just as quickly. His head spun as the wound flared hot, then hotter, overpowering the agony of the poison inside him.

"What else have you done, *inimicus*?" Jude asked, almost sweetly. "What other foul deeds have you committed against the humans of this earth?" He leaned closer until his breath huffed over Dee's ear, cold as ice. "Submit yourself to penance, little one. Tell us your sins, so we can cleanse you."

Dee cried out, desperate and hopeless. He tilted his head back, silently begging Dominic to slit his throat and send him to oblivion. Ilya could not reach him here. Not even Dara could reach him here.

"I ... I-I at-tacked a Virtue," he sobbed.

Dominic hesitated. "You attacked ...?"

"My rescuer," Dee said weakly, eyes fixed on the knife poised above him. "Sh-she – she moved too quickly and I … I panicked, I didn't mean to, I didn't *mean* to, b-but I lunged at her and … and bared my teeth …" He whimpered softly as his fangs pressed against his lower lip. "I didn't mean to," he whispered. "I j-just wanted to protect my … the human. I th-thought she was … I didn't *know* …"

Dominic laughed. "You bared your teeth at one of the holiest of us, after she removed you from our retribution? You truly are a *vile* and ungrateful creature." He gave Dee a wicked grin as he plunged his knife into his exposed abdomen again.

"*NO!*" Dee shrieked, arching away from the blade as it cut deep inside him. The pain crescendoed and he turned his head, heaving again. Nothing came up but a weak trickle of blood.

"I knew this one was wicked," Jude said with a gentle smile. "But I had no idea how deep the corruption went." His fingers left scorched hair in their wake. The smell burned Dee's nose, and he shuddered.

Still, the fire in his blood was subsiding, slowly. It gave way to the agony of the wounds from the knife. He trembled and shook, sweating through his clothes.

"What else have you done, *serpentis*?" Lucas said, nudging him with his toe. "Surely there is more."

"Y-yes," Dee gasped, beyond all thought, beyond anything but the pain inside him. "I …" His eyes filled with tears. "I-I corrupted the … the human."

Dominic let out a breath through his nose. "Well, we could have told you that." He grinned as he leaned over Dee and slid his knife into him once more.

Dee's scream was weaker now. He shuddered with relief when Dominic pulled the knife back again. The smell of his blood was thick in his nose, metallic, tinged with fear and something else, something like burning flesh. He lay motionless under Dominic, save for his heaving chest and trembling lips. His throat bobbed as he looked up toward the single lightbulb hanging over him.

"I ... I s-somehow m-manipulated them," he rasped. Guilt and grief crushed his heart. "I ... I don't know how, but ... th-they care for me, I'm unworthy and they *care* ..." His throat constricted in an animal whine. "Th-they are – are *good.*" He squeezed his eyes shut, trying to brace for the knife.

For a long moment, no one moved. No one breathed. Dee cracked his eyes open and stared at the angels, one by one, as they loomed over him. His hands were numb beneath him.

"*How* deeply do they care for you?" Dominic said, staring down at Dee. His hand hovered in the air, knife still dripping blood onto Dee's shirt.

The back of Dee's neck prickled. He shivered as sweat chilled his skin. "Wh-what, angel?"

"I said ..." Dominic smiled and plunged the knife into Dee's stomach. Dee screamed his throat raw. "How. Deeply. Do. They. Care. For. You?" With each word, he twisted the knife harder. Dee's vision went white and he writhed under Dominic's weight. He coughed, and blood speckled his lips.

Dee's mouth bobbed open as he tried to speak. *They feel for me. They care about me.* He could barely draw breath past the shard of fire inside him. His eyes rolled back and he tried, desperately, to focus on the angels above him who spun with the rest of the room.

When his eyes finally focused on Dominic, his blood ran cold. The angels were looking at each other, with identical expressions of vindication on their faces.

"So you have poisoned yet *another* human soul," Lucas said with satisfaction dripping from every word. He looked down at Dee with a snarl on his lips. "You have damned another life to the flames."

"N-no," Dee breathed, shuddering as his own blood cooled on his skin. He screamed as Dominic jerked the knife out of him and sealed the wound shut with his burning hand.

"We must save the sinful human that tethered their soul to this creature," Jude hissed through his teeth, lips pulled wide in an inhuman smile.

"N-no, *no!*" Dee sobbed. His voice broke. "No, merciful angels, *no*, they – th-they are innocent, they are blameless, it wasn't their f-fault – "

He cried out as Dominic backhanded Dee across the face with his empty hand. Dee felt himself bleeding inside, felt the bones in his shoulder grind and grate. His face was glazed with tears as the angels all stood and stepped away from him in one fluid motion. The room hummed. Dee felt the vibration deep in his bones. He sobbed, open-mouthed, and tried to drag himself to the angels' feet with his hands still cuffed behind him.

"P-please," he breathed, blind with dread. "No. Please. Not Ilya. Please not Ilya."

Lucas laughed and kicked Dee hard in the stomach. Dee screamed and shuddered as agony ripped through his wounds.

"This will be *fun*," Jude said, looking down at Dee. He reached down and grabbed a handful of Dee's hair to yank him upright. Dee cried out and shuffled to his knees. "It is the Lord's will to eradicate the stain on the earth that you create, little snake. No matter. This will only take a little time."

Dee's eyes were wide as he screamed his horror.

11

— ◦ —

"Lucas, would you like to fetch them, or do you want one of us to do it?" Jude said with a vicious smile on his face. He glanced at Dee and smiled wider as Dee sobbed.

"I think I'll do it," Lucas said, turning back to grin at Dee. "This will only take a moment." Dee blinked tears out of his eyes, and Lucas was gone.

"*NO!*" Dee shrieked, gasping past the collar that seemed to constrict around his neck. "No, *no*! *Ilya*!" Tears streamed down his face and he collapsed to the floor, sick with horror. "*Ilya ...*" he whimpered, eyes wide and sightless as he lay limp on the cold ground.

Jude stepped forward and gripped what was left of Dee's hair. "Now you *and* your little friend can submit yourselves to penance," he crooned, looking down at Dee with gentleness that made his skin crawl. "We truly are doing the Lord's work today."

"N-no," Dee sobbed brokenly. Agony lanced his heart. *Not Ilya. Not Ilya. Not Ilya.*

Dominic snorted as he glanced down at Dee. "Should have thought of this before you corrupted them, little snake," he said, his lip curling. "'It is joy to the just to do judgment: but destruction shall be to the workers of iniquity.'"

"B-but they are not iniquitous," Dee whimpered against the floor. "They are innocent, th-they are *good* – " He screamed as Dominic kicked him in the stomach again. His eyes rolled back and he gagged weakly against the stab of pain through the knife wounds.

"Quiet, *daemon*," Dominic sneered. Dee heaved a shuddering sob. He pulled against the iron cuffs, even as the bones in his shoulder ground together.

There was a *thud* upstairs, then a scuffle against the floor. A muffled voice raised in a shout of fury. The sound of an open palm against flesh.

Dee moaned as he dragged himself up to his knees again, eyes fixed on the basement door. His heart clenched and he nearly retched as pain burrowed deep into his wounds. He trembled in every limb, his skin on fire with terror and guilt and grief. The basement door flew open, and Lucas dragged Ilya heavily behind him.

Ilya raged against his grip, aiming kicks at Lucas' legs. Their hands were bound behind them, and they shrieked through the gag tied around their head. A bruise marred their cheek. Blood dripped from their nose and into the gag.

Ilya. My Ilya.

"*No!*" Dee sobbed, tears streaming down his face. Ilya's eyes went wide and they lurched forward in the angel's grip, screaming through the gag in their mouth. Lucas jerked them upright and dragged them down the rest of the stairs. He forced them to their knees just outside the line of the Trap imprisoning Dee and yanked their head back, his fingers tangling in their tight curls.

Ilya's eyes swept over Dee, taking in the blood that stained his shirt, the burns on his face, his hair singed short now, the way his arm hung loosely in its socket. Ilya raised their eyes to the angels standing around them and snarled their rage.

"Hello, little one," Jude said gently, lips curving into a sickly smile. "So you are the human that this one has so thoroughly corrupted." He nudged Dee's chin and grinned when Dee flinched away from the burning touch.

Ilya trembled, their eyes fixed once again on Dee. Tears stained their cheeks and wet the gag. Their jaw worked around it and they whimpered softly, all their fury gone and replaced with horror.

"I-Ilya, *no*," Dee whimpered. His body was gripped with cold terror, and he shivered. The angel's blood still seared in his veins. Sweat poured down his back and soaked his shirt.

Dominic stepped forward and reached for the cuffs on Dee's wrists. Dee cringed away from him, ducking his head and whimpering softly. With one touch, the chain on his wrists fell away. Dee threw his head back and screamed as Dominic wrenched his arms forward and passed his hand over the cuffs again. Fire flared through Dee's shoulder as the chain locked his hands in front of him. Still, he sagged, dragging in breath after breath of relief. His shoulder wasn't twisted quite so terribly this way. He swayed on his knees, dizzy and trembling from the pain stabbing through his abdomen.

"Go to them," Jude said gently, nodding toward Ilya. "Go to the one you corrupted, *daemon*. Look into their eyes and see that you have brought them to their death."

Dee's head snapped up. "*No*," he croaked. "No, merciful powers, no, *no*, please, they are innocent, *please*, kill me, not them, please, *please* ..."

Ilya cried out wordlessly and shook their head against Lucas' grip, eyes wide and desperate. Their gaze was locked on Dee, just as he was unable to look away from them.

"The wages of sin is death, little snake," Jude murmured. "You know that. Their life was forfeit the moment they let you into their heart. It is wickedness, to love something wicked."

Dee desperately shook his head. "Please," he breathed.

"**Go to them**," Jude commanded.

Dee and Ilya both flinched away from the thunder of his voice. Dee lurched forward on his knees, but before he could cross the small width of the Trap, Jude kicked him to the floor. He convulsed and screamed, curling around the wounds in his stomach. He cradled his arm, grateful – so, so grateful – that he had his hands again, even if they were still shackled. The command crushed his bones, tugged at his limbs, and he dragged himself forward, sobbing as every movement sent jagged agony stabbing through his shoulder.

He crawled until he could feel the edges of the Trap under his skin like an electric current. He collapsed to the floor in front of Ilya, pressing his face against the cold cement in supplication. He splayed his hand out against the floor, reaching, reaching, fingers going numb as he forced them closer to the edge of the Trap.

"Ilya," he whispered. "*Ignosce me, carissime Ilya –* " [*Forgive me, dearest Ilya –*] He grunted as Dominic kicked him hard. Ilya screamed and thrashed against Lucas' grip.

"K-kill me," Dee groaned, helpless. "I-I will – will take the punishment for my sins. But please ... do not punish them. I will – will take the punishment, I will take the knife, just *please*, do not hurt them ..." He bit down on his tongue as Lucas threw his head back in a peal of laughter.

"You are not in a position to bargain, little one," Lucas said with a chuckle. "Yes, you will take the pain, you will take the punishment. You have no choice in this. We do the holy will of our Lord. But this one, this precious little thing that you turned away from the path of righteousness and took down the path of evil and sin ..."

Dee forced himself to look up. Lucas had one hand fisted in Ilya's hair and the other gently cradling their face. Ilya glared up at him with rage in their eyes.

Lucas smiled gently. "This one will also pay the price. This is the pursuit of true justice, little snake. Sometimes it is fierce. Sometimes it is born through pain. But it is always glorious. 'If thou do that which is evil, be afraid; for he beareth not the sword in vain: for he is the minister of God, a revenger to execute wrath upon him that doeth evil.'"

Dee's stomach dropped as Lucas drew his blade and held it to Ilya's throat. Ilya went still, their eyes wide and brimming with tears as they looked down at Dee in stark terror.

"*No*," Dee sobbed. He could barely form the word past the horror clogging his throat.

"Their life is the price of your sin," Lucas murmured. His gaze pinned Dee to the floor. "And you will watch them pay the cost."

Dee let out a wordless scream of agony as Ilya began to sob.

12

—·—

"Ilya," Dee breathed, muscles shuddering as he tried to force himself through the Trap. It was like pushing against an electrified fence, the current jolting through him and locking his muscles into agonizing rigor. He wept sulfurous tears and threw himself against the Trap again.

Ilya was mumbling incoherently through the gag, tears streaming down their face and into the now-soaked fabric. They struggled against Lucas' grip and cried out when Lucas grabbed a handful of their hair and twisted it viciously.

"L-Lucas, *please*," Dee sobbed, pressing his forehead against the floor. "I-I'll do *anything*. I'll ... You can – you can f-flay me, like you said, or – or hang me, or – "

Ilya's scream silenced the words in Dee's mouth. He looked up, stomach heaving, but Lucas was not hurting them – Ilya was staring at *him*, eyes wide with horror. They desperately shook their head. Tears cascaded down their cheeks and onto the floor.

"P-please," Dee rasped. "Lucas ... *please.*"

Lucas smirked. "Beg if you must, creature," he said with a grin. "Beg, scream, cry, but their fate is tied to yours – and their fate is sealed." He looked down at Ilya and reached for the gag. "Confess, little one," he murmured. "Confess your sins before we surrender you to judgment." He pulled the gag from Ilya's mouth.

"*No!*" Dee wailed.

"*D-Dee,*" Ilya sobbed, taking in hitching, gasping breaths. "Dee, I'm so sorry, Dee, *no* ..."

Dominic snorted and stepped forward. Dee flinched away as Dominic's boots stopped near his face. "*Dee*? That's what you've been calling it? Dee as in *demon*?" His lips twisted and he kicked Dee hard in the stomach. Dee shrieked and curled into himself, retching against the pain. "What a dark joke to play," Dominic said as he pinned Dee under his boot.

"He's not an *it*!" Ilya shrieked. Their face was flushed red, shining with their tears. They trembled in Lucas' grip, even as Dee tried to force his hand through the Trap again. Dominic kicked Dee onto his back and laughed at Dee's scream.

Jude's lips quirked into a smile. "Oh, it's a *him* now too, is it?" he crooned. He knelt by Dee's side and dragged him upright by his collar. Dee gagged and choked as it closed around his neck. "The human seems to want to treat you as if you were human, too." Jude looked at Ilya, and Ilya shrank back against Lucas, trembling under Jude's gaze. "Just how debauched are you, little

67

one? Did you take him to your bed? Did you love him, lie with him?"

"*No!*" Ilya cried. They wet their lips and glared at Jude. "H-he never wanted that!"

Dee's stomach lurched and he shook his head, eyes streaming as he choked, shuffling on his knees. He could not meet Ilya's eyes. His cheeks would have burned with shame if he had a heartbeat. It was true; all he'd ever wanted – and all Ilya had ever done – was to be held, cradled, soft hands rubbing his back and soft lips resting against his forehead. Acid clawed its way up his throat and he gagged on his panic.

Jude huffed out a laugh. "Well. At least there's *that* small mercy." He drew one finger across Dee's throat and chuckled when Dee screamed and tried to twist away.

Dee swallowed and tasted bile at the back of his throat. "Th-they are human," he heaved, head spinning with the pain. "They – th-they are – are *human*, it's not like with me, th-they are … Their s-soul is still pure, *please* – "

"Nothing is pure that has love for you," Dominic said with a vicious sneer. He stepped forward and struck Dee across the face.

Dee whimpered as blood streamed from his lip. "P-please, angels, *no!*" he sobbed. "Please, please, l-let them go, h-hurt *me* … not them …"

"Some things are unsalvageable, little snake," Jude said almost sadly. "They were lost the moment you arrived in their life.

It is regrettable, but ..." Fingers combed through Dee's short hair. "They are damned to the flames."

Ilya whimpered and heaved a broken sob. Dee reached out and gasped when his fingers again hit the edges of the Trap. His shoulder was on fire. He could scarcely breathe.

"At least their list of sins is short," Lucas sighed. He untied the rope from around Ilya's wrists. Dominic stepped forward to help as Lucas forced Ilya's hands together in front of them and tied them, palm to palm. He clutched their hair and forced them onto all fours in front of Dee. Dee thought he would be sick from the terror in Ilya's eyes, the tears that trembled there, unshed. His throat clicked as he swallowed. His lips were numb.

"I-I'm sorry," he breathed. Ilya whimpered. Then he heard a sound, one so familiar that he knew it in his bones. He looked behind Ilya and saw that Lucas had stepped back and uncoiled a whip, letting the end *smack* against the ground. He whined wordlessly, the collar seeming to choke him again. Tears poured down his face. His abdomen flared with pain.

Dominic pulled Ilya's shirt up until it bunched around their shoulders, exposing their back. He tucked the hem of the shirt into their neckline and stepped back.

"This will not take long, little human," Lucas said, his voice placid and calm. "Punishment for the sin of loving the wicked creature in front of you, and then ..." He shrugged. "You will die, and we will continue our work."

69

"N-no," Ilya sobbed. They reached forward, and their hands passed through the Trap as if it wasn't there. Dee lurched forward and clutched their fingers, knuckles going white. He was shaking so hard he felt like he would fall to pieces. Ilya squeezed their eyes shut.

"No, look at it," Jude murmured. Ilya opened their eyes and stared up at Jude, panting, trembling. Jude shook Dee by the collar. "Look at it. This creature is your downfall, little one. Look into its eyes as we deliver justice for your sins."

Ilya brought their gaze to meet Dee's. Their lips trembled and their mouth fell open with a sob.

The first lash came down, and Ilya screamed their agony.

The sound split Dee in half. He lunged against Jude's grasp. His fangs flashed and his eyes blazed, pupils blown wide with fury. "*Invocabo maledictum super te, damnnatus potestates –* " [*I invoke a curse upon you, damned Powers –*]

A blow snapped his head to the side. He pitched onto his broken shoulder, smashing his head against the cement floor. The room spun around him and he blinked against the ringing echoing through his head. It took him a breath to realize the sound was Ilya screaming.

He blinked, slowly, half-blind with pain. His body felt boneless. He couldn't move.

Jude dragged him up to his knees again and grabbed his face. Dee roared as his skin blistered under the touch, smoke from his own burning flesh choking him as Jude pried his jaw open. Each time he tried to reach up to pull the hand away, his shoulder exploded with pain.

"I thought we told you not to use that language or else we'd cut out your wicked tongue," Jude rasped in Dee's ear. Dee could see Ilya kneeling in front of him, being held back by Dominic as they raged and fought to get to him. He squeezed his eyes shut, willing his head to stop spinning. When he opened his eyes, they still would not focus.

Even under the searing agony of the angel's touch, he felt a trickle of warmth down his neck. He shuddered and froze when the smell of his own blood overwhelmed him. It was streaming from the cut on the side of his head, soaking his hair and staining Ilya's shirt more.

He weakly tossed his head, trying to shake free of the angel's burning grip on his face. He fell perfectly still when the cold blade of Jude's knife pressed down against his tongue. It pricked, and blood welled in his mouth. Jude released his face and clutched his collar instead, keeping the knife in Dee's mouth, almost touching the back of his throat. Dee gagged and winced as it only cut his tongue deeper.

Dee forgot the knife when his eyes finally focused. Ilya was on their knees in front of him, taking deep, gulping breaths, hands bound and braced against the floor. Each exhale was a sob. And Dee could smell their blood – clean, not like his at all. His fangs flashed and clinked against the knife in his mouth.

"Continue," Jude said with a smile. Dee raised their gaze to Lucas. Lucas grinned and wound up for the next swing.

"*N-n –* " Dee coughed as the blade slit his tongue and more blood pooled in his mouth, dripping from his lips.

Lucas brought the lash down, and Ilya's scream tore Dee apart. Dee's tears stung the burns on his face. He sobbed weakly, choking on the collar and the knife in his mouth. Blood streamed down his temple and matted his hair.

Dee felt the next lash as if it had landed on his own back. He wailed with Ilya and sobbed when they met his eyes. Jude braced Dee's head back against his chest and stroked his fingers down Dee's cheek. Dee writhed and burned under the touch.

"This is the price of your corruption," Jude whispered in Dee's ear. "Look at the agony you have caused in this human that thought they could trust you."

Dee screamed against the knife as his heart shattered in his chest.

13

—◦—

Ilya's back was a mess of blood. It streamed down their sides in rivulets, staining the cement beneath them. Dee's head spun with the scent of it. He gagged weakly on his own blood, and on the knife that Jude kept firmly between his lips, pressing down on his tongue. His eyes burned and streamed with helpless tears.

Ilya wailed as another lash came down. They sagged against the ground, barely able to hold themself up under the whip. They took great, heaving sobs, their head bowed toward the floor.

"Please," they cried. "Please, no!"

"*I-Il –* " Dee gagged on the knife and tried to reach for them with his hands chained together, shoulder wrenching as he did. They raised their head to look at him. He felt shame like a knife to his heart when he saw their tears, the snarl of agony written across their face, the way their bound hands trembled against the floor.

"Almost done, little one," Lucas said softly. "Almost done."

Dee roared his rage and lunged forward against Jude's hold. He sobbed and choked when the knife pressed down harder against his tongue.

Lucas raised his gaze to Dee, his lips pressed together in something that looked almost like *sorrow*. "Just a little more punishment for your fallen friend," he murmured, tilting his head at Ilya. "Then we surrender them to the flames, and continue our work with you."

"N-no, *please*," Ilya sobbed. They trembled in every limb as they looked back at Lucas, wincing as it pulled on the lash marks on their back. "P-please, please don't kill me, don't ... Please don't kill *him* ..."

Lucas tsked and lowered his arm. "Don't worry, little human," he said softly, and hardness found its way into his eyes again. "You will be reunited again – a few decades from now, after we have finished punishing our little snake."

Dee screamed and coughed on his own blood. *Ilya isn't damned. Ilya isn't going to Hell. Even once the angels are finished with me, I'll never see Ilya again.*

"D-Dee," Ilya whimpered. Dee's eyes were wide, black taking up almost the entire iris, fangs bared and flashing in the light. He couldn't look away from Ilya. Blood trickled down their arms, pooling on the floor in front of them. They reached out, flinching and sobbing as the muscles twitched in their back. Their hands slid along the floor, reaching past the Trap and toward Dee. Dee struggled and tried to clutch their hands. They were too far away.

Crack.

Ilya screamed and crumpled to the floor, half in the Trap and half out. Their blood smeared on the ground.

"Come on, Jude, let them be together," Dominic said as he watched Ilya writhe in pain. "The little creature is the human's downfall. At least let it touch what it has broken."

Jude rolled his eyes and slid his knife out from between Dee's teeth. Dee winced as it sliced the inside of his mouth. "Fine," Jude huffed. "But once the human is dead, I want the demon's tongue." He shoved Dee to the ground.

Dee cried out as the bones in his shoulder crunched. He lay motionless on the floor, room spinning, stomach heaving. He cried out and flinched away from a gentle touch on his arm. When he could finally get his eyes to focus, he saw Ilya, sprawled out on the floor beside him, desperately reaching for him with their bound hands.

"Dee," they whispered. Their voice cracked. "Dee."

"I-Ilya," Dee murmured. The sound was slurred, twisted by Dee's bleeding tongue. "I'm s-sorry."

"I l-looked for you," Ilya sobbed. They shuddered and hissed out a breath through their teeth. "We tried to find you, Dee. We knew ... I couldn't let them *h-hurt* you – "

"I'm sorry I brought this pain on you," Dee croaked. "F-for-give me, Ilya, *carissime Ilya, ignosce me ...*" [*dearest Ilya, forgive me ...*]

"N-no," Ilya sobbed. "No, *no ...*"

Dee and Ilya screamed together as the lash fell on Ilya's back again.

Dee shrieked and bared his fangs at Lucas, eyes blazing. He was too weak to stand. He could only lie on the floor with Ilya, their blood mingling at the edges of the Trap. He wrapped one hand around theirs and held tight.

If there is a H   eaven like I've been told, and not just a Hell after this ...

He could not bear to think any more.

"Last one, little one," Lucas said softly. "Dominic, put them on their knees again for me, would you?"

Dominic snorted and stepped forward. He fisted a hand in Ilya's hair and dragged them upright. Ilya's hand was ripped from Dee's grasp. Their blood smeared against the floor as Dominic put them on their knees just outside the Trap.

A pit opened up inside Dee like a clap of thunder.

Where a moment ago he'd been trapped, pinned inside the circle by an unseen force, now he could feel the downward pull toward Hell inside him again. He could smell sulfur in his nostrils, could feel the unearthly heat of his home against his skin. He could feel how he rattled around inside the body, hardly tethered to it at all. There was another body here, one with a pounding heart and a pure soul, and his mind cried out for him to leap inside the fresh body so when they both died, he could latch onto them and ride that tether into Hell.

He would become nothing if he died in this body.

Dee trembled, gasping, as the thunder rolled through him again and again. He'd so quickly forgotten how it felt to be free of the Trap. He blinked against the tears that blurred his vision and raised his head, looking for the source of the newfound power.

Ilya knelt in a smear of their own blood, shaking and sobbing, their eyes squeezed shut in anticipation of the final lash. Mingled in with the blood was a streak of the Trap's white paint, moistened and smeared against the floor.

The circle was broken. It was enough.

Dee raised his head to stare at the angels around him. He could not fight his way out, not now. There was no escape. No escape but death. And to escape death now, he had to rend himself from this body and enter Ilya instead. It called to him, a fresh body with only the whip marks to cause it pain, inviting him in to look through their eyes and feel through their skin, a pure soul to tie himself to. He would have to drag them to Hell with him in order to survive.

Dee's stomach lurched. He clenched his jaw so hard his teeth ached. *Never. Never again. Not to Ilya.*

Upstairs, there was a *bang.*

Everyone froze.

Lucas tilted his head toward the ceiling. "Hm. Go see what that was, would you?" he said breezily. Jude and Dominic both nodded and headed for the stairs.

Dee lay still with bated breath, not even daring to look up. If the angels saw that the circle had been broken, they gave no sign. Jude and Dominic climbed the steps and opened the basement door. They disappeared into the silence upstairs.

A scream pierced the air. The house shook in its foundations.

"*Damn*," Lucas spat. He jerked Ilya back by their hair, dragging them backward until they fell against his chest. They clawed at his hand but went still when his knife pressed against their throat.

"*Thy will be done*," Lucas murmured, and pressed the blade in.

Dee shrieked and launched forward with strength he didn't know he possessed. He passed through the line of the Trap as easily as the angels had. He pried the knife away from Ilya's throat, screaming in agony as his broken shoulder twisted. His skin burned like an open flame as he tore Lucas' hand from Ilya's hair, taking whole curls with it. He shoved Ilya behind him and lunged again at Lucas, mouth open, fangs bared, growling like a cornered animal.

"*Tu nolo adtracto eos*" [*You will not touch them*], Dee roared, feeling flames lick along his skin. Drops of blood fell from his lips and steamed when they hit the ground.

Lucas' eyes flashed. His mouth pulled into a wicked grin as he adjusted his grip on the knife. The edge was marred with Ilya's blood.

"*Ego ire necare tu, daemon*" [*I am going to kill you, demon*], Lucas sneered.

"*Tum ego ire adigere tu ad infernum mecum*" [*Then I will take you to Hell with me*], Dee snarled, and lunged forward.

Lucas swiped at Dee, and Dee staggered back. His body was ablaze with agony, every breath, every movement sending fire racing along his limbs. He lunged forward again and gripped Lucas' wrist. He screamed as his hands blistered. Lucas grabbed at Dee's hair, but his fingers slid right through the short strands. Dee snapped his teeth in Lucas' face, inches from tearing skin. Lucas jerked his head back. Dee tightened his grip on Lucas' wrist and forced his hand back with a burst of strength, slicing the knife through Lucas' throat.

Lucas' blood poured over Dee's hands like a fountain. Dee let out a twisted scream as Lucas grabbed his arm with his free hand. Dee's skin blackened, angelic blood streaming down his forearms, burning everything in its path. Lucas stared at Dee with shocked, empty eyes.

Lucas swayed. He looked down at his hands, one holding Dee's arm, one holding the knife covered in blood. Dee's strength was fading. He clung to the angel, half-leaning on him as Dominic's blood still burned through his veins.

There was a whimper behind him, and Dee's heart plummeted in his chest.

Ilya.

Dee glanced behind him, desperate, sick with terror at what he would see. Ilya lay on the floor, wrists still bound, one hand pressed to their throat. Blood spilled out between their fingers. Their eyes were wide with terror and their shirt covered their back once more.

A boot scraped against the floor. A flash glinted in the corner of Dee's eye.

Dee's breath was punched out of him, a half-formed plea on his lips as agony lanced through his chest. He was only vaguely aware of the angel collapsing to the floor in front of him, holy blood spilling out of his body until his eyes went empty and dead.

The cacophony upstairs had ceased, too.

"I-Ilya," Dee croaked, and turned to face them. They were staring at him in horror, tears falling from their chin and streaming down their neck.

They weren't looking at Dee's eyes. They were looking at the knife, buried to the hilt in his chest.

14

Dee's throat worked, again and again, as he stared down at the hilt of the knife in his chest. He felt the blade like a shard of ice buried deep inside him, piercing the heart that lay silent within him. Tears rolled down his cheeks and he took a staggering step toward Ilya. They lunged at him with their hands still bound in front of them, the wound at their throat forgotten, as he collapsed in their arms.

"N-no," Ilya mumbled, eyes wide with panic. "N-no, *no*, Dee, *no* ..." Their hands shook as they closed around the handle and jerked the knife out of Dee's chest. He let out a strangled whine and slumped in Ilya's arms, limp and trembling and cold. Ilya dropped the knife to the floor with a clatter that made them both flinch and did their best to cradle Dee in the circle of their arms.

"No, Dee, *no*," Ilya breathed. Their lips trembled as they looked him over, tears falling freely now, mouth twisted, voice breaking. "No. No no no no. Dee, *no*."

Dee's chest heaved with rattling breaths that took more and more strength with each gasp. He whimpered as he felt the floor leaching his body heat through his clothes until it felt like he was lying on a slab of ice. Ilya's hands fluttered over him, brushing the last long strands of hair away from his face, clutching at his hand, cradling his cheek in a palm stained red with his blood. Dee shivered and looked up at them. They were blurred with his unshed tears and with the fog that was slowly closing over his vision.

A warm wetness soaked his shirt. He blinked, forced himself to focus. Blood was spilling down Ilya's neck and chest from the cut at their throat, unheeded and forgotten in their panic. Dee reached up, shaking, his hands still cuffed together. Ilya ducked into the touch and his fingers brushed their cheek, but he shook his head and pressed his hand against the wound instead. Their blood felt inhumanly warm, compared to the icy cold of his fingers.

He knew he would feel cold. The blazing heat of his home didn't call to him anymore.

"P-please, *no*," Ilya sobbed. "No, Dee, I'm so sorry, *no* ..."

"Ilya," Dee breathed. "*Carissime Ilya*" [*Dearest Ilya*]. His arm shook as he tried to keep his hand pressed to their wound. "*Fortasse in aliam vitam*" [*Perhaps in another life*].

"Wh-what?" Ilya whimpered. They held him tighter against their chest. "Dee ..."

Dee's eyes rolled back. He couldn't feel his lips. The slice of agony that had pierced his heart was fading now, dulling to a flat, metallic weight in his chest. He whimpered softly, his eyes streaming, as he tried to find Ilya. He could feel their warmth, could feel their arms around him, but that was fading, too.

"*No!*" Ilya cried as Dee's hand grew cold against their neck. "Dee, please don't ..." Slowly, slowly, his hands slid down their chest, leaving a smear of blood in their wake, to fall limp in his lap. His head fell back and he heaved one more tortured, wheezing breath. Then he was still.

15

—·—

Ilya folded over Dee, wracked with sobs, and wailed against his shoulder. "*Dee!*" they screamed. Their throat spasmed shut. They coughed and gasped for air. "*Dee, NO!*"

"**Ilya!**"

Ilya was nearly thrown backward by the force of the voice. They looked up, tears streaming, at the figure standing at the top of the stairs, shining like a star made human. They whimpered and cringed away, holding Dee tighter to their chest. His body was growing colder by the second.

The figure dashed down the stairs and screeched to a halt, falling onto their knees in front of Ilya. The light emanating from the figure faded until Ilya could just make out the angel's face.

"Dara!" they shrieked, sick with hope, their heart hammering in their chest.

"Oh, god, *Ilya*," Dara cried, reaching out and brushing her fingers against the cut at Ilya's throat. It sealed immediately, leaving no scar. Ilya blinked and realized Dara's face was spattered with blood. Her clothes were soaked in it. She touched the ropes at Ilya's wrists, and they fell away.

"D-Dara, *Dara*!" Ilya sobbed. They clutched her hand. "Dara, h-help, *help*, Dara, he's ..." Ilya cut themself off with a broken sob.

Dara had gone very still at Ilya's side. Ilya's stomach lurched as they finally got a good look at her face, her light faded enough now that she no longer hurt to look at. Dara was staring at Dee with fathomless sorrow written across her features.

For a long moment, Ilya couldn't speak. They felt cracked open, flayed alive, crushed under the weight of their anguish, looking down at Dee's face as he lay perfectly still in their embrace. His head hung limply over their arm. His eyes were still half-open, his face blank – empty. His body felt ice-cold against Ilya's skin.

"*NO!*" Ilya screamed, rocking Dee back and forth, heart aching at the weight of him in their arms. "D-Dara, please, please, *fix him* ... Y-you, you fixed *me* ..."

"No, Ilya," Dara said gently. Her voice was husky and rough.

"*Please!*" Ilya sobbed, and grabbed her hand. "Dara, *please, please*, heal him, h-he ..."

"I can't, Ilya," Dara murmured. She bit her lip as she looked at Dee. "He's ... he's dead. He's gone."

Ilya stared dumbly at Dara. Their skin felt like it was ablaze, save for where Dee felt freezing in their embrace. Ilya's hand shook as they gently cradled Dee's head.

He seemed so *small*. His right arm hung oddly from his shoulder, and his face was marked with burns in the shape of the angels' fingerprints and hands. His hair was almost completely singed away, leaving only a few patches of short, uneven strands – and blood soaked the hair that was left, staining his temple and neck. The fountain of the angel's blood had burned Dee's hands and forearms. The front of his shirt was marked with more blood – his and Ilya's. When Ilya peered closer, they saw that there were holes in the shirt over Dee's abdomen. They stared, uncomprehending, at the tiny rips in the cloth.

Not holes. *Stab wounds.*

Ilya lurched to the side and gagged weakly. Dee slid further onto the floor, and Ilya clutched him tight, holding him in their lap as they sobbed.

"Th-they hurt him so much," Ilya wailed. "Dara ..."

The angel made a strangled noise in her throat. "I kn-know," she whispered.

"They ..." Ilya sniffed, then flinched, pain shooting through the whip marks they had all but forgotten in their desperation. Dara's mouth pinched as she lifted the back of their shirt and passed her hand over the wounds, soothing the pain and mending the torn flesh.

"Th-they told him he was ... was *wicked*," Ilya whimpered. "They t-told him he was – was s-sinful and h-had c-corrupted me ..." They heaved a wracking sob and crushed him against their chest, pressing their forehead against his so hard it hurt.

They squeezed their eyes shut and struggled to draw breath. "Th-they were – were punishing him ... for *me* ... and me for him ..."

"I'm so sorry," Dara rasped. The sound cut Ilya to the bone. "I'm so ... so sorry I let them get to ... to *both* of you. I never ... I never could have imagined they would be so goddamned *brazen* ..." She curled her hand into a fist, shaking the house in its foundations. She blew out an icy breath and released her hand. The house settled. "I'm so sorry."

Ilya raised their head and saw Dara with her hand stretched out, inches from Dee's face.

"*NO!*" Ilya shrieked, and clutched Dee tighter against their chest. Dara froze. "No, d-don't – don't *touch* him ..." They swallowed bile and couldn't tear their gaze away from the burns that marred Dee's face.

"He's gone, Ilya," Dara said, the sound barely a breath. "I can't ... I can't hurt him anymore." She reached out and drew her fingers gently across his cheek. His skin didn't blister; it stayed unbroken and whole. Ilya looked up at Dara with confusion furrowing their brow.

"He doesn't live in this body anymore," Dara murmured. Her voice broke, and she cleared her throat. "There's nothing here now that I can hurt."

Ilya sobbed weakly and held him close. "Wh-why is he so cold?" they whimpered.

Tears glittered on Dara's eyelashes. "He was driving around a ... a body, Ilya. A body that wasn't ... alive. What you felt ... the warmth that came from him was – "

"Was his fire," Ilya croaked. They pressed their lips to Dee's forehead, their tears falling into his hair.

"Yes," Dara said softly. She pulled her hand away. Her fingertips were stained with his blood – or from the blood of the angel Dee had killed to keep Ilya safe. Ilya's gaze strayed to the ring of worn and blistered skin around Dee's throat and wrists, and the iron cuffs and collar that had burned him. Their stomach heaved, and suddenly they could barely stand to look at Dee.

"T-take them off," Ilya croaked, shuddering. "Th-the – the cuffs. And the ..." They rocked forward with a broken sob. "Th-they put a *collar* on him again!"

Dara moved with speed that made Ilya's head spin. She tapped her finger against the iron locked around Dee's neck and wrists. The cuffs and chains fell away and clinked to the floor. Ilya snatched them up and hurled them across the room until they hit the still, silent body of Lucas – the angel who had taken Dee. Rage burned in Ilya's belly.

Dara followed their gaze. Her eyes flashed, and sparks danced across her skin. The earth groaned beneath them, so low Ilya could feel the vibration in their chest.

Another deep inhale, another deep exhale. The earth fell still again.

"I-is he in Hell?" Ilya whispered, tamping down the tendril of hope that dared to swell in their chest.

"No," Dara said with finality. Ilya's eyes fell shut and they nodded, rocking Dee and shivering as their own blood cooled on their clothes. "No, he ... he is truly gone. It has not often happened, but when a demon passes through the veil with no human soul to ..."

Ilya crumpled and muffled a sob in Dee's shoulder. Dara trailed off into silence.

Ilya nodded, over and over, as they held Dee. "They killed him," Ilya croaked. "They *killed* him." Ilya found Dee's hand and squeezed.

Even so, as they wept, they could feel the emptiness of the body. Without Dee inside it, there was no warmth, none of his goodness, none of his life. Without Dee, the body was a stranger to them.

"They killed her, too," Dara growled. "They showed neither any mercy. Just as they showed you. They did not even ... mean to kill her. I don't think they considered her for even a moment."

Ilya's throat bobbed. Every beat of their heart felt like a throb behind a bruise, pain with no relief. They could not bear to let go of Dee, could not bear to feel him leave their arms for the last time.

"Wh-what happens now?" they whimpered. The basement seemed to grow even colder around Ilya.

"We bury him," Dara murmured. The air carried a crackle of electricity, humming with the inescapable current of the angel's sorrow. "We tried to find the human's family when we first found Dee, me and Evangeline." A single, crystalline tear rolled down her cheek. It evaporated before it hit the ground. "We never did. I ... I don't know who she was or where she came from."

Ilya whimpered, and the pit inside them only grew. They held Dee's hand to their face and brushed their lips against his knuckles. His hand felt limp and cold – and dead.

"I'm sorry," they whispered, and crumpled over him again. "I'm so ... *sorry*. I ... I love you, Dee. I love you." Their throat tightened, and they couldn't speak. They knew he couldn't hear them, wherever he was – because he was gone, truly gone, not unreachable but *gone*. Ilya tipped their head back and wailed their grief. Their voice echoed oddly against the cement walls and floor of the basement. When they felt Dara's cool arm around them, they leaned against her and wept into her shoulder.

"Come on," Dara said gently. "Come on, Ilya. Let's get you home."

"Dee," Ilya whimpered, holding him tight. "Dee."

"Let's go," Dara said, a little more insistently. "Eva's keeping watch upstairs. And once we leave, she ..." Dara tilted her head back, as if staring through the ceiling into the floor above. "She's going to fucking *smite* this place from the face of the earth."

Ilya's throat bobbed as they looked down at Dee's face. Ilya didn't know what was worse – the slackness there, the emptiness, or the burns that marked his skin. Slowly, slowly, they closed his eyes and rested their forehead against his temple.

"Okay," they croaked, flat and despairing. "Let's go."

Dara wound her arms around them both, hiding her tears. She closed her eyes – then the basement was empty, save for the knife, the iron, the dead angel, and the smears of Dee's blood on the floor.

16

Dee woke up choking on smoke. He rolled to his side, heaving forward, his lungs aching like they were on fire. He clutched at his chest – and at the knife that had pierced his heart. The knife was gone. And beneath his ribs, a heartbeat thrummed, hummingbird-fast with pain and fear. He swallowed thickly and reached for the collar that he had died in.

Gone. His wrists were free, too.

He blinked ash out of his eyes and scrubbed his face. Tears left tracks in the grit on his cheeks. He shuddered and realized his body was bathed in sweat, oppressive heat crushing his skin and forcing its way down his throat. The smell of sulfur burned his nostrils. He coughed and reached for his abdomen, bracing for the stab of pain through the wounds left by the angel's knife.

Nothing. No pain, no blood, no wounds.

Trembling, he raised his head and dared to look around.

A thunderclap of relief broke over him and was quickly swallowed by terror. He cringed away from the dust that blew into his eyes and blinked against the blinding roar of fire in the sky. He could almost feel his lungs blister from the heat. He gagged and clawed at his throat, whimpering, head reeling with confusion and pain.

"K-Kiernan?" croaked a wavering voice behind him.

Dee cried out and scrambled away in the dust, only just now realizing he was naked. He covered himself, squinting through the smoke at the shadow that stood before him – just a shadow, no flesh, no bone. He swallowed and winced at the sandpaper feeling in his throat. His lips felt cracked, almost too dry to speak.

"Eligos?" Dee rasped.

The shadow flew toward him and he flinched back, throwing his hand in front of his face. Disbelief fluttered in his chest. His shoulder was restored; it was like it had never been broken. For the first time, he looked down at his body, and saw that it was not his body at all.

The last body had never been his either, though.

"Wh-what's happening?" Dee asked before he doubled over in a fit of hacking coughs, trembling on hands and knees.

A touch like a tendril of fire licked over his jaw, his cheek. His eyes watered, but he lifted his head and tried to focus on the shadow in front of him – one that bore a face he knew so well. *Had* known for so long.

"You are corporeal," his friend breathed.

Dee groaned as the heat from the sky above singed the hair on the back of his neck. "H-hotter than I remember," he murmured with an uneasy twist of his stomach. The ground baked against his skin.

Why am I here?

Why am I alive?

"You did not have a body, last time you were here," Eligos whispered. Dee could barely hear him over the hot, screaming wind. "Did you go to Earth, my friend? Did you see the colors, hear the music, eat the humans' food?"

Dee raised his gaze to Eligos' and braced against the memories of the knife, the whip, the holy water. He shivered despite the heat and rubbed at his neck.

The shadow drifted back, and Dee could feel the sorrow radiating off his friend. "You were found," Eligos murmured.

"Y-yes," Dee said, choking on the word. "I was found, and … and taken. I w-was held." Sweat stung his eyes.

"Where?" The word was barely more than a breath in the wind.

"I don't know," Dee moaned, and he slumped forward, baring his back to the blazing sky. "In a dark place. A basement. By three angels – Powers."

His friend gasped, and Dee felt a touch like fingers through his hair.

"But I was … I was saved." Dee raised his head. Tears ran from his eyes. "I was saved. A human … they took pity on me. And … two Virtues – "

"You were held by *Virtues*?" Eligos gasped. The tendril of touch in Dee's hair retreated. "Kiernan – "

"P-please," Dee whimpered. "Do not ... don't call me by that name. The Powers, they ... they made me ... recite that name, made me say it as they drowned me in holy water ... They carved it into my skin, over and over, then let me heal enough so they could do it again ..." He let out a shuddering sob and reached out toward the shadow that was his friend. "Please."

"I ... I am sorry," Eligos said softly. "What do you want me to call you, friend?"

"Dee," he murmured. His tears evaporated on his cheeks. "Just ... Dee."

Dee swore he caught the flicker of a smile in his friend's shadowy face. "Alright," Eligos said.

"But the Virtues did not hold me," Dee murmured. "They did not ... hurt me. They ..." Dee could barely get the words out past the lump in his throat and the fire in his lungs. He longed to claw the prickling, stinging skin on his back. "They cared for me. But ... the human most of all."

Eligos was silent for a long time. "I have never heard of such a thing," he said finally, his voice desiccated and dry.

"Neither have I," Dee said brokenly. "I had ... I had a few days, at most, in the body I found. And then I was taken."

"Y-you've been gone for *years*," Eligos said gravely. "That whole time ..."

"Most of it," Dee said. "Most of it was ... under their penance."

A sound like the roar of a forest fire tore from Eligos. Dee flinched away, scrambling backward on his hands. "What they do is not *penance*, Kier – Dee. Even their Lord does not call for torture. He calls for death, if he calls for anything." The shadow spat sparks, and Dee squeezed his eyes shut against his friend's sudden anger, shifting to his knees in the burning earth. His friend's anger passed over him like a wall of fire, then flickered, faded.

Dee shivered as Eligos stood perfectly still before him. Then, slowly, Eligos reached out and let the shadow of his hand pass over Dee's shoulders. "You are changed," Eligos said softly.

"I kn-know," Dee whimpered, cowering against the ground.

"No," Eligos murmured, and guided Dee's head up until he met his friend's eyes. "You are ... you are not of this place anymore," he breathed, his touch brushing Dee's face like smoke.

Dee's throat bobbed. He was desperately thirsty. He looked down at his hands, and they were peeling in the blazing heat. He swallowed hard and met his friend's gaze.

"What have they done?" Eligos whispered.

"They killed me," Dee whimpered. "They ... p-put a knife in my heart."

"But what did they do *first*?" said Eligos. His gaze burned Dee's skin. "They have done ... something."

Dee whined softly as he looked into the depths of his friend's eyes. He felt it all, the whip, the knife, the iron, the water, the crack of his own bones –

– the burn of Dominic's blood in his veins.

His hand flew to his throat, but there was no wound there, no scar. He trembled as he remembered how it felt, the fire creeping through his veins and searing him from the inside out.

"They gave me their blood," he croaked.

The shadow of his friend twisted and keened in his shared pain. "*No*," he gasped. "That must have been – "

"Torture," Dee whispered, and shut his eyes. Even his tears burned him. "It was torture."

"And you died with it ... still burning you?" Eligos said.

Dee opened his eyes and looked up. The blazing sky felt imprinted on the backs of his eyes. "Yes," he murmured.

His friend's scalding shadow swiped the tears from Dee's cheeks. "Then," Eligos said, voice quavering, "you know you cannot stay here."

Dee folded forward with a sob. "I know," he whimpered. "But I cannot return to earth, I ..." He clutched at his hair. It was long enough to grab now, curling past his ears and against the nape of his neck. "Th-they will hunt me."

"But you will burn here," Eligos said. Dee felt the too-hot touch encircle his wrist. "See?"

Dee couldn't pull away. The prickling heat of his skin under the touch of his *friend* was too much like the agony of the angels' clutches. He was frozen, staring down at the shadow that held him with a fiery grip. He whimpered and pressed himself lower against the rocky ground. The stones ground into his knees and burned him there too.

"Go," Eligos said with a groan. "Go, my friend. Find the human, or find your solitude. You can live on Earth. But ... carefully. Perhaps in secret." He lifted Dee's face. "This may be difficult to hide."

Dee blanched. He licked along his lips and winced when his fangs pricked his tongue. He had not meant for them to come out, had not tried to show them in his pain or fear – they were there, part of him. He shuddered and swallowed hard.

"Your eyes, as well," Eligos murmured. The shadows around his own eyes deepened. "Still slitted. Like they always are."

Dee whimpered softly. If he looked like what he was, unable to hide even his fangs behind the subterfuge of human teeth, he would end up right where he'd been – or worse.

I had decades more penance to pay. Dee whimpered again, louder. His flesh felt like it was melting off of him slowly.

"Come," Eligos said above the howling wind. "Come. You cannot stay here. The blood that ran in your veins was never meant to last here. It may be why you burn still."

Dee was so, so tired of burning.

He struggled to his feet, blushing at his own nakedness. Even wearing the human woman's body had not made him feel so exposed, but this was *his* flesh, *his* blistering skin.

Still, even the fire of the sky above him and the burning grit beneath him was nothing compared to the agony of the angels' touch, of holy water in his lungs, of angel's blood in his veins.

"Wh-which way do I go?" he croaked.

"I don't know," Eligos said sadly. "I know only fire, and that is everywhere." The sky flared above them, and the shadow of Dee's friend seemed to waver.

Dee reached out and let the shadow touch his palm. "Thank you," he whispered, eyes streaming from the heat and from the sinking feeling in his heart. "Thank you, for – "

A gust of wind and sand that scoured skin from Dee's body swept over them both. Dee cried out and fell to his knees, protecting his nose and ears. The sand felt like sparks falling on his back. The air felt like the inside of an oven. He sweat, and he panted, and he burned.

When the wind faded he stood up, casting a glance up at the inferno sky. He was utterly alone on an empty, blasted plain, swallowed by fire and heat.

He picked a direction, and started walking.

ABOUT THE AUTHOR

Isaac Ryals is the award-winning author of the dystopian series *Honor Bound*. His achievements include Reader Views Literary Awards winner in the LGBTQ+ category, Next Generation Indie Book Awards finalist, Reader's Favorite Awards five-star seal, and The Wishing Shelf Book Awards Red Ribbon award. His short fiction and poetry have been featured in *Erato*, Z Publishing's *Colorado's Emerging Writers* and *America's Emerging Poets*, and *High Grade*. He works at a university and moonlights on an ambulance as a paramedic. He lives in Illinois.

You can follow Isaac online at:
  https://whump-tr0pes.tumblr.com/
  https://archiveofourown.org/users/whump_tr0pes/works

BEFORE YOU GO

This is the first book in 12 Months of Whump, a series of whumpy novellas published by WPP throughout 2025. Each novella can be read as a standalone.
To stay up to date with the 12 Months of Whump series and other whumperfly-inducing projects, visit us at
https://thewhumpyprintingpress.tumblr.com/